THE MOBILE BAKERY AT THE CHRISTMAS PARADE

Jodie Homer

Copyright © 2024 Jodie Homer

This novel is a work of fiction. Any names, characters, businesses, places and events are a product of the author's imagination or to be used fictitiously. Any resemblance to actual persons, living or dead, or actual events is purely coincidental.

Copyright © 2024 Jodie Homer
Cover By Richard Homer
All rights reserved

CONTENTS

Title Page

Copyright

Summary

Acknowledgement

Other books by the author

Chapter 1	1
Chapter 2	8
Chapter 3	14
Chapter 4	20
Chapter 5	26
Chapter 6	32
Chapter 7	41
Chapter 8	47
Chapter 9	52
Chapter 10	58
Chapter 11	64
Chapter 12	75

Chapter 13	83
Chapter 14	91
Chapter 15	99
Chapter 16	110
Chapter 17	119
Chapter 18	130
Chapter 19	139
Chapter 20	147
Chapter 21	155
Chapter 22	162
Chapter 23	170
Chapter 24	177
Thank you	185
All about the Author	187
Social Media	189
Trademark Acknowledgement	191
Magical Christmas on the Isle of Skye - Chapter 1	195

SUMMARY

Twelve years ago, April left her childhood friend and boyfriend Ben to follow her dreams of being a famous baker, but now she is coming home with her tail between her legs. Ben is still upset about April leaving, so when she comes back he wants nothing to do with her. When April and Ben get thrown into organising the Christmas parade together, can they put their feelings and twelve-year feud aside for the sake of Christmas and give the villagers a parade they will never forget?

ACKNOWLEDGEMENT

It's that time again where I roll out the names. So I am going to start with the people I live with, mostly my husband who designs my covers for me actually and always takes my photos holding my books when I nag him to. I also want to thank Becky for her patience, I'm sorry I can be so bad at this and you are constantly reminding me of the things I should know. I really should write them down, and thank you for formatting my book too and creating some of my pretty pictures with my covers. I also want to thank the support of Bettina, Jaimie and a new author I've discovered called Luna. They are always at the end of Facebook when I need to ask something or if I'm having a really bad writing/editing day and also Anita and the Chick Lit and Prosecco group for being virtual cheerleaders to all the writers in the group and supporting everyone. Lastly, I want to thank everyone who reads my books, reviews my books and shares my posts I make on SM I really appreciate it.

OTHER BOOKS BY THE AUTHOR

Raindrops on the Umbrella Café

A Magical Christmas on the Isle of Skye

Married By Thirty

A Village Called Christmas

Meet You in the Summer

CHAPTER 1

I can vaguely hear 'Lonely this Christmas' playing in our canteen as I nervously shuffle my feet. We are waiting for our fate like pigs at the slaughter. Will we lose our jobs today? I've been a cake maker for birthday cakes at Milly's Cakes for twelve years-ever since I came out of school and became an apprentice.

"April Jones, Sarah Hancock and Will Scott, will you come into the office?" Jane pops her head around the door and gestures for us to enter the main office. Sarah is one of my close work friends; she took me under her wing when I was a fresh-from- school apprentice. She's been like a work mum to me, but of course no one replaces my real mum. My heart starts thudding when I think of home, Birchlea-Heath village, and our little cottage, Rosie Cottage. I don't go home as often as I would like to and that hangs over me like a thunder cloud.

"Why don't they just line us up and shoot us? It would be less humiliating," Will says, stubbing out his cigarette before joining us.

"You've been here longer than me, you should definitely get to stay," I say reassuringly to Sarah.

She flashes a smile to me but it isn't full and it doesn't make her green eyes sparkle behind her red-framed glasses.

I've always dreamt of running this place with Sarah.

"Come in and sit down," Jane says, gesturing for us to sit on the three chairs she has put in a line in front of her desk. I sit down on the one near the little window and wait. I feel my heart thudding. *Please don't fire me today not so close to Christmas.*

"We've had a hard couple of years and, as you know, business hasn't quite been the same as it used to be. So we have to make the company smaller to save it," Jane says.

I feel my hands shaking. I do know the business hasn't been the same. We aren't taking as many customer requests as we used to. I used to be busy making a cake every day sometimes, but now we are lucky if we get a customer once a week.

Jane straightens her green blouse and looks at us.

"I'm really sorry for bringing you in here and putting all of this stress on you all but I'm afraid I can't keep you all on any more." Jane sits down and puts her manicured hands over her head.

I don't know why she is so stressed. She isn't getting sacked a month before Christmas. What will I do for Christmas? Where can I go?

"You are free to stay for the rest of the day, but after that I'm sorry but you're not needed. Tomorrow, you will get your pay plus four weeks of leave pay," Jane says and, just like that, we are dismissed.

I walk back into the bakery but when I see the candyfloss pink walls I don't feel excited. My heart sinks. I moved away twelve years ago, away from my best friends and parents. I've put my heart and soul into building my life up. I even rented a grotty apartment. I was saving up for a nicer place but I work a lot and spend my free time posting to social media about my cakes. And all I have to show for it is a measly redundancy packet I have to live on for god knows how long.

"Are you staying for the day?" John asks, putting on his coat.

"I don't know," I say feeling numb. I feel like I've just broken up with the cake shop. It's worse than seeing my teenage boyfriend Ben's face when I left after I finished school. My stomach knots again when I think of that. I haven't really thought about Ben in years. Could I go home? Would that solve everything? I look around one last time and get my coat. I definitely don't want to stay for the rest of the day. I put my coat on and walk out of the bakery forever.

❖ ❖ ❖

"Really, Jimmy," I say standing outside of my flat which I seem to be locked out of. I have my hands on my hips with all of my things thrown onto the front lawn.

"I told you I'm selling up. I gave you notice. I'm sorry," Jimmy says, throwing another bag out of the front door.

I'm not sure why he thought he could come into my house and pack my bags for me.

"I have always paid the rent on time. I have kept the flat clean and I have had the worst day of work ever," I say. I feel a spot of rain and my shoulders sag. I don't need anything else going wrong right now.

"I need to sell up, April. I can't afford to rent out to you any more," Jimmy says and stubs out his cigarette. I sigh as I drag my bags to my car. My car's definitely seen better days.

I watch Jimmy on the phone as he lights up another cigarette and curse in my head that he chokes on the bloody thing. I start my car and on the second try it starts up. People stop and turn as my car rumbles into existence.

What a fucking day. I switch on some music and the heating as I prepare for my journey, but where can I go? I look in the backseat. Basically my whole life is in this car right now. How did everything go so wrong? I should be a famous baker by now, the Nigella of baking or whatshername who won bake-off a couple of years ago.

I huff as the radio plays way too jolly Christmas music for my mood and subconsciously start heading towards Birchlea -Heath village.

Do I want to go home and grovel, with nowhere to live and no job? I feel like I've failed at life already and I'm only thirty-two. I reach the roundabout. The sign to the left reads: 'Welcome to Birchlea-Heath village.'

My mum's coffee shop is two minutes away and something inside me makes me excited to be back home. I didn't think I would get that feeling coming home. I drive past the little school on the left. My best friend, or should I say old best friend, works there as the head teacher. Opposite Brew and Chill-mum's cutesy coffee shop -is the garage that Ben worked at before I left. As I approach the blue and yellow building, my stomach twists.

I reach a crossroad. Ahead I can see both buildings and I'm not sure which one I'm more nervous to approach first.

◆ ◆ ◆

"Well bloody Nora, look who's come through the door?" My mum gives a customer their drink and comes to greet me.

"Hi, Mum," I say breathlessly as she squeezes the

life out of me.

"So are you staying for Christmas? Do you need some food? Come and sit down." Mum doesn't wait for me to answer, but just sits me down on the leather seats next to the huge window where I can keep an eye on the garage opposite.

Mum fusses around me. "So why are you back?" I'm instantly interrogated and I tell her all about me losing my job.

"Oh April, I'm sorry." Mum gets up and throws her arms around me.

"Need me to take over, Mum?" my big sister Emily asks. Mum nods and my sister waves to me.

"Is it alright if I stay here? I will get a job, I promise, and I will pay my way," I say.

"You can work here," Mum says and I take off my coat and scarf.

"So do you still make those beautiful cakes, Ape?" Emily asks. I hate that she still calls me that after all these years.

"Yes, but I lost my job so I don't think I'll be making cakes anytime soon," I say.

"That's a shame, like Mum says you can always help us here and I'm pretty sure most of us will be pleased you are home," Emily says.

I shiver when she says *most of us*. I know exactly who she means when she says 'most of us.' I wonder if he is still here. Ben Thomas. My best friend from primary school and my first boyfriend. We were together until we were eighteen and I got an apprenticeship at a cake shop and we had a huge argument. He said I was selfish for taking it and I called him selfish for holding me back. I feel a shiver running up my back when I remember him saying he never wanted to see me again.

CHAPTER 2

"Want to help me decorate the Christmas tree?" Mum asks when Emily goes to see Dad across the road at the post office.

Mum knows how much I adore Christmas. Or at least I did until I lost my job but I can't really say no now.

Mum has already cranked the music up and I look into a cupboard labelled 'staff' where a box of Christmas decorations sits by the door. I drag it out.

"Do you remember us making this for Mum?" Emily asks. She is back from giving Dad a drink and is helping me with the tree. She shows me two old clay hand print decorations we made when we were at school.

"Yes, why does Mum still have all of this?" I ask.

"Because I cherish the things you made when you were little," Mum says, stringing the Christmas lights onto the tree with Emily.

"Yeah but did you need to keep everything?" I ask, seeing a manky framed picture of toothless me in a Santa hat as a child.

"Of course, I think it makes the tree look more personal," Mum says.

We start hanging the decorations around the tree. The embarrassing photo ones we put more around the back and the star one Emily made in nursery where most of the glitter has fallen off near the top. We dance around to the Christmas CD Mum put on as we finish and I can't help but feel really Christmassy.

When we are done, we share a packet of bourbons with our coffees at the table.

"I missed you, Mum," I say, suddenly welling up. I should have come home more often. I should have invited them to my flat. Why did I want to get away from my life when I had Mum and Dad right here… and Ben Thomas?

My heart sinks again at how we ended everything. I don't think we can even be friends any more. So much was said during that argument. Even though it was things said in the heat of the moment, it's things that can't be taken back.

"I missed you too, honey. What's brought this on?" she asks, raising an eyebrow. She isn't daft. She probably knows exactly what I am thinking.

"I don't know, just all my feelings of being back

here. It's made me miss this place, you and Dad," I say and huff.

"And someone else too?" she asks.

"No Mum," I say.

"You know it isn't too late to apologise. It will make you feel better. And he's clearly over it," she says. She hands me a brown bag. "Take this to your dad, he likes having a cookie with his coffee."

I take the bag, wondering what Mum meant by that, and cross the road to the post office.

Dad is sitting behind the counter with a stack of parcels on the left of him. Christmas music is coming out of the stereo.

"Well blimey, look who it is. Could it be my other daughter?" Dad says, positioning his glasses on his face. He comes over and hugs me.

"Yes, Dad, I've come home," I say. I ignore the feeling in my gut that's telling me I should never have left and put the bag down next to Dad's drink.

"Well, I'm very pleased to see you," Dad says and gives me a pat on the head. Since I was younger, Dad's affection has pretty much been a pat on the head. It's comforting and it makes me wish again I hadn't left. I really screwed up. I look out the window at the garage next door. There's a car parked outside so I know it's still running.

"He's still there, you know," Dad says.

"Mum said he was and that he doesn't care about what happened," I say hoping, he'll tell me what that means.

I see Dad's mouth turn up at the corners. "No, he seems happy now. Why don't you go over and say hello?"

Dad makes it all sound so easy. Just go over to the man I loved. The man whose heart I had broken who now seems fine. I don't think I will be saying hello to Ben Thomas.

"No Dad it's okay," I say.

"You were friends for years. You should at least go and say hello." Dad pats me on the head reassuringly again.

I can't help but think back to that terrible day everything went wrong.

◆ ◆ ◆

4th May 2011

"April, have you ever thought about marriage?" Ben asks.

I only have a short time with Ben. We are sitting in Brew and Chill, sipping iced lattes. I choke on my drink as my brain scrambles to come up with an answer.

"Urm, Ben we are only eighteen," I say. Most girls

might have thought about their wedding days but not me. I am going to own my own bakery. I will be a top celebrity baker on one of those cosy BBC shows on a Sunday morning.

"*I know but when you know you love someone and want to spend your life with them,*" *he says and stops.*

I sip my drink, wishing my taxi would come and we could just hug and see each other at the weekend.

"*April,*" *Ben says, getting down on one knee. Oh shit. "I love you, I know you want to leave but surely there will be other opportunities closer so we can be together? Please, April, don't leave. We can make this work.*"

He shows me a ring in a box and I feel anxious. I bite my lip. I know it's our last day but I didn't expect this. I wonder if Dad and Mum knew about it. Is everyone trying to find reasons for me to stay? Why can't they realise this is a great opportunity for me?

"*Ben, I'm sorry but I have to take the chance. I have to take risks and see where this apprenticeship will take me,*" *I say. I look at his face and he looks devastated. Was getting in a relationship the wrong thing to do? Will I lose my best friend now?*

"*But we could have an amazing life here,*" *Ben says.*

"*What, in this boring village where nothing happens? I would be stuck here Ben, I would be miserable,*" *I say.*

"*Is that what you think of me? Boring?*" *he asks, his voice barely a whisper.*

"No, but I think you are selfish for trying to hold me back," I say. In my head I'm thinking: why did I say that? I have attracted a bit of a crowd now. I notice my mum watching us. Will they agree with me or Ben?

"I think you are selfish for throwing our relationship away for what -an apprenticeship?" he says, raising his voice.

"It isn't just an apprenticeship. If you had any ambition at all you would understand," I say and instantly regret it

"Wow, I can't believe you just said that. I have ambition. I am going to be owning my own garage soon and what will you be doing? Making cups of coffee for your boss because you aren't actually good enough to own your bakery. You live in a fantasy world and you wonder why you didn't get a place in college," Ben shouts.

I feel the venom in his voice: My body is shaking with anger. I want to run away forever. I run out of the coffee shop and into my now waiting taxi. I look out of the window and see Ben staring back at me. I won't ever forget what he said.

CHAPTER 3

My stomach knots as I leave the warmth of Dad's post office, staring at the peeled paint of the blue and yellow garage. The rain drizzles on me as I instead cross the road and head back into the coffee shop.

"Oh My God," comes the voice behind me in true Janice from Friends style. She even does the nasally voice and I whip around. My best friend -or old best friend - is standing at the door. She looks like she's been dragged through a hedge backwards but it is definitely her with her unruly red hair.

"Till," I say, running to her. She throws her arm around me.

"I can't believe you are back," she exclaims and steps inside the coffee shop. Her hair is damp from the drizzle that can't decide if it wants to be rain or snow.

"I know, neither can I, but apparently bakers aren't needed as much nowadays," I say with a shrug.

"Ouch, so what are you going to do?" she asks and orders a coffee from my mum. I sit down opposite her.

"I don't know yet, I'm just so glad to see you all. I've missed you," I say.

I feel guilty I haven't stayed in contact. I've seen Tilly's updates on Facebook, like when she got her teaching job, but that's it.

"So what happened with your apprenticeship?" Tilly asks.

"I worked so hard for years before I got my job at Milly's Bakery and then we were called into a room and basically let go. That's twelve years thrown down the drain," I say and sigh. It isn't like I'll get another job so close to Christmas.

Mum comes over with a coffee for me. "You girls catch up quickly because they are going to do the light switch on in"-she checks her watch -"forty minutes."

I always loved the Birchlea-Heath light switch on. It used to be outside the butchers next to the garage but I already see crowds of children and parents all around the garage. The street lights are now on and it's getting dark.

"I think you will be stolen from us quicker than the Grinch stole Christmas. You are an amazing baker and I'm so fucking glad you are back." Tilly reaches over and squeezes me.

"Till, you can't swear, you're a teacher," I exclaim.

"I can fucking do whatever I fucking want to and if I want to sit with my old bestie and drink fucking coffee then I fucking will," she says and I giggle. Some things never change and I definitely wouldn't want them to.

"I'm pleased you still want to know me. After what happened, I was sure you would agree with him and I guess after all these years he was right," I say. I won't admit it to him if I see him, though.

"I'm really sorry I didn't visit. Work has been mad and, well, I didn't want Ben to think I had abandoned him," Tilly says.

"You mean like I did," I say. I sip my coffee, looking at the crowds in front of the garage.

"No, of course not, but Ben needed someone when you left. I mean, I don't blame you for going," she says.

"I had to figure it out for myself. I wanted to get out there and I did. Until last year we were doing amazing and now... Well, now I am jobless and I lost my friends," I say.

"You haven't lost me. Maybe I should be annoyed you left but I'm too nice," she says and I laugh. She hasn't changed at all.

The door opens and I hold my breath as Ben walks in. I don't realise I'm clutching my mug so tightly until my knuckles turn white. I look at Tilly who looks from Ben to me.

"Shit, I didn't think he would come here," I whisper. I want to cringe into my seat as Ben turns around and looks at me.

He looks exactly the same except for a few more lines on his forehead. His blond hair still short now. I meet his eyes and cringe into my seat. Ben moves a hair from his eyes nervously.

"Hey Benzie," Tilly says with a smile. Ben doesn't take his eyes off of me and a shiver runs down my spine. I don't need an answer. Ben Thomas still hates me.

"Benzie?" I ask. Even I never called him that.

"I told you we stayed friends when you left," she says.

"Oh, hey Tilly," he says, completely ignoring me as if I'm not there. He hovers next to Tilly.

"Hey, you remember April, don't you?" she says, gesturing to me. "She's back for Christmas."

"Hi Ben," I say, trying to keep my voice normal. I don't know why I am nervous. He said horrible things as well as me. We are both guilty.

"Yeah," he says as uninterested as he could possibly sound.

Mum comes over to clean the table.

"You should all get yourself out there for the light switch on," Mum says.

"Yeah, see you there," Ben says and gets his coat on, ready to leave.

"See you there," Mum says. I don't say a word.

"I'm only staying to be Santa and then I have to MOT a vehicle in my garage. Nice seeing you Till," Ben says. Mum shakes her head, mumbling to herself, and leaves.

I watch after him. "Ouch," I say to Tilly.

"Yeah, he's still pretty angry you left him," she says.

"I'm not too happy with how we left things," I say.

"You both need to sit and talk about it," she says. "Get it all out."

I scoff. Yeah right that is the last thing I want to do. Instead, I head behind the counter, pull out a mixing bowl and turn the radio up a few notches.

"Ooh, you're baking. Is this your stress baking again? Remember when you were hung-over and you made all those little cupcakes for me and Ben?" she asks.

"Yes and no, I'm not stressed, I just thought I would get into the community spirit," I say, mixing ingredients together with Mum and April both surrounding me.

"Oh April, I am so pleased you are back. I haven't been able to bake a lot. We've had to order our cakes and biscuits in now because of my hands," she says.

"I don't mind making them for the shop," I say, stuffing the mixture into the oven. I wash my hands at the sink.

"See, you are sort of following your dream," Tilly says.

"Oh honey, I'm sorry it didn't all work out, but you know you can stay here at the shop as long as you need to," Mum says.

I feel awful. Mum has clearly got the world on her shoulders. She has lines where I don't remember there being lines. And the bags under her eyes are bulging. Her hair, once dark brown, now has grey sprinkles in it.

"Thanks Mum," I whisper and hug her.

"You know, I don't think I ever told you how proud of you I am for getting yourself out there," Mum says.

"I'm also proud of you," Tilly says, joining in the hug. "You got away from this village to do something with your life."

"Yeah and that turned out amazing," I say sarcastically.

"Who cares if it didn't work out," Tilly says.

I smile. With my best friend and mum to support me, who cares if Ben Thomas hates me? I am not exactly his biggest fan. All I know is I am home and they say home is where the heart is.

CHAPTER 4

Mum closes the shop and Tilly and I carry the mince pies over to the little gazebo where crowds are building up.

"Welcome home, April," Mr Thomas says. He doesn't seem to hate me for leaving his son.

"Thank you, Mr Thomas," I say and smile back as I put the mince pies down.

"You know you can call me Neil," he says.

Mr and Mrs Thomas, Neil and Dawn, are the councillors of the village and organise all of the events. They've also always encouraged all of us to attend the meetings to have our say.

There are crowds gathering as the rain turns to sleet and falls around us. The ground below us is wet and slushy already and the temperature has dropped. I see my breath as we gather around the cluster of shops that have the unlit lights hanging over them.

A car arrives on the corner of the road. "Ladies and gentlemen, I want to introduce Andy, our local radio presenter. He is going to turn the lights on for us," Neil says.

"Hello, hello, villagers how are we doing?" Andy says way too enthusiastically.

Mum comes over with a mince pie and a little white plastic cup of mulled wine.

"Get this down you, keep you warm," she says and I take it. I'm not watching Andy doing the Macarena with half of the villagers before the switch on starts, I'm looking through the crowd to see Tilly standing next to Ben and a girl. Is this his girlfriend? Tilly catches my eye and smiles and I slowly make my way over.

"Trust the weather to go shit now," Tilly says. She throws her arm around me and already smells slightly of mulled wine.

"Hi, you must be April, I'm Paige," Paige says and smiles nervously at me.

"Hi, Paige. I'm so pleased I'm back in time for the switch on," I say.

Ben scoffs and moves his hair out of his eyes. Classic Ben move. He used to do this when he was nervous. Is he nervous to see me?

"You should have come back for the others," he says.

I roll my eyes. "Don't you have to go and be Santa or something?" I say.

"Yep," he says turning away from me.

"Can we all be nice?" Tilly asks.

"I was just saying," Ben says.

"Ben shush, I love this switch on and you are ruining it," Paige hushes at him.

"Go and be Santa and take your mood somewhere else," I say.

"At least I have a job," he says.

"Bloody hell Ben," Tilly says.

"You know what, I don't need to hear this from you," Ben says and leaves with Paige, who looks completely confused.

"He doesn't mean it. He is clearly still angry you left," Tilly says.

"I don't care," I say with a shrug. I saw him move his hair out of his face. If this is his front and he is actually nervous then all I need to do is ignore him.

"Okay then, well let's forget about Ben and enjoy tonight," Tilly says, taking my hand and swaying while Andy sings Christmas songs badly into a microphone. I wrap my coat tighter around me with my other hand as the sleet falls on us.

When Andy finishes butchering 'It's Beginning to Look a Lot Like Christmas' Tilly lets go of my hand.

"I will be back. I'm a part of the school choir tonight," she says and goes to join the group of children on the little stage next to the gazebo. I stand on my own and watch as Tilly starts singing and the children join in.

"I've missed you," Emily says, appearing next to me. She pulls her hat further down her ears and we both watch the choir.

"I've missed everything," I say, feeling that guilt again.

Emily looks at me. "Yeah but you are here now, so don't worry about it."

"I just wish I had stayed in touch when I left," I say. So many regrets that make my heart thud. I've let everyone I love down.

"I know, sometimes I want to leave this boring village and go and explore but I don't have the guts to," Emily says.

"You?" I almost choke.

"You think I want to spend my life working with my mum in a coffee shop?" Emily says.

"Well I tried it and it didn't work out. The grass wasn't greener for me," I say.

Emily nods and takes a sip of her mulled wine. I do the same and I wait for her to answer.

"That's what worries me. I want to be around for Mum and Dad and to see you of course, but I really want to meet someone I didn't go to school with," Emily says.

"This village is lacking decent men," I say. I look around and see a few faces I went to school with- and of course Ben who now hates me and is all loved up with Paige.

"Mum doesn't understand it. She keeps trying to set me up with Matt."

"I remember Matt the prat from your year," I say and pull a face. Matt was the school prankster. I haven't seen him in years but there's only so many times you can pull his finger and laugh at him. He might be different now.

"He's still gross, I saw him picking his nose when he was trimming his mum's grass," Emily says.

The microphone starts squeaking and a car comes slowly down the road, blasting out 'Christmas Vacation.'

"Ho, ho, ho!" The kids all run up to the car. Santa greets them all and tells a couple of jokes.

I walk over to Tilly and stand with her.

"Can I join you?" Paige asks, standing next to us.

"Sure," Tilly says. We watch Ben walk onto the stage dressed as Santa. "Ben's dad made him volunteer to be Santa after last years Santa died."

"Is everyone ready to start counting?" Santa asks.

"Ten, nine, eight, seven, six, five, four, three, two, one," we all shout and the row of shops- including the post office and garage- light up with pretty fairy lights dangled across them. We all cheer, looking up at the lights that are speckled with sleet.

"Thank you everyone for coming out. I will hand you all back to Andy as I am busy sorting out presents for Christmas. Now, make sure you are all good little boys and girls," Santa says and the children wave as Santa is driven off.

Andy steps back on the stage to entertain the crowd and I go to find Mum who is handing out mince pies with Dad sat on a deckchair next to her.

"April, there you are, your mince pies are selling like, well, mince pies," Mum says with a smile.

"That's great Mum," I say and smile.

"Well done kiddo," Dad says through mince pie crumbs.

I feel a warmth inside me that I didn't feel when I worked in a bigger bakery. It's strange that being home is bringing back all of these feelings-but definitely not for Ben. Even if he is helping be Santa, he has still been mean to me since I came back. I look around at the villagers eating my mince pies and realise that maybe I lost my job for a reason. Maybe I was meant to come back here again and figure it all out. The cold and sleet hasn't affected my mood at all and I go home in my mum's car feeling happy yet exhausted.

CHAPTER 5

"Hello sleepy head."

I feel something hitting my face and wake up. Emily's face is so close to mine it's blurred.

"Cup of tea girls?" Mum shouts up the stairs.

"Yes please," Emily answers for me.

"Don't you understand personal space?" I ask Emily grumpily.

"Nope," Emily says. "You need to get up, Mum's opening Brew and Chill and she says she would like you to make some more mince pies before we open."

I groan and turn over. I feel something cold pour onto me and scream. Emily is standing over me with a cup of water.

"Come on, up," she says. I wonder sometimes who the big sister is in this family.

I reluctantly get up, my wet hair sticking to my face, and walk downstairs.

"She's up, Mum," Emily shouts to Mum. The back door is open and I can already see the rain coming down.

"Good, Emily take a cuppa to your Dad, you know what he's like-pottering in his blooming greenhouse again."

"Morning Mum," I say, yawning.

"April, if you could get down to the coffee shop soon and start on the mince pies, that would be great."

"Yes Mum," I say. I sit down in my chair and pour myself a bowl of Coco Pops. Mum potters about the kitchen.

"So you are actually going to be baking at the shop? It's a good thing you've come back. I have tasted the cakes Mum orders and they aren't very nice," Emily says.

"I did try my best but you can't beat home-made," Mum says.

"Yes, I will see how it goes. They say things happen for a reason, don't they?" I say hopefully

"Yeah but that's usually to make themselves feel better," Emily says. "Anyway, I will see you at the shop." She leaves me to eat and get dressed on my own.

Still tired, but dressed at least, I pick up my black umbrella. The walk to the coffee shop is only five minutes and the moon is still out.

It hasn't stopped raining the whole way. The wind is frosty and when I open the door, the warmth from inside is welcoming. I peel off my wet mac and close the umbrella.

Emily is cleaning the tables and I flick on all the coffee machines.

I get started on my mince pie mix, turning up the radio as I go and making Emily roll her eyes. She really needs to get more into the Christmas mood and, now I am back, I will make sure she does.

"Do you have to do that so early?" Emily says, sitting down with a drink already.

"Yes, it's a month until Christmas which means I can let out my Christmas side," I say, flinging my arms around as Mariah hits that long last note. Besides, the village is already Christmassy, so why shouldn't I be?

I put my batch into the oven and look out of the massive front window. The sun is slowly coming up, well I say sun, it's more foggy and grey. The rain has finally let off, leaving puddles outside.

I prepare myself for the queue of early morning customers

◆ ◆ ◆

"Fancy some lunch?" Tilly asks as soon as she

walks in. She takes off her scarf and coat and sits next to the window.

"Yes," I say. Mum has come in to cover my break.

I make myself and Tilly a drink and go and sit with her.

"So how are things here at the minute? Has Ben come in to talk to you?" she asks.

"No he hasn't. How come no one told me Ben had a girlfriend?" I ask.

"I don't know really. I've been busy with school and Christmas before we finish the term," Tilly says.

"I guess it doesn't really matter. I'm here and back just in time for the fayre," I say.

"There's rumours that the town fayre is being cancelled as there just isn't enough interest in it," Tilly says rubbing her temples. "Will you come to the meeting at four?"

"Will Ben and Paige be there?" I ask. Silly question really. Of course they will. He is the son of the councillors.

"Yes," she says biting her lip. "April, if you are staying here, you are going to have to learn to live in the same village as them."

"Of course she is going." Mum appears and gives me a look. I gulp down my coffee and my stomach feels unsettled. Can I really just ignore Ben? How long will he play this game for? Surely he can't keep up the front.

The door opens and Ben walks in with oil stains on his clothes. Tilly gives him a smile and wave and I look out of the window at the very uninteresting grey sky.

"Talk about the man and he appears," Mum says and gives me a side glance. I look up and meet Ben's eyes. Why should I feel bad that he has come into my work place?

"You were talking about me?" he asks in more of an accusing tone.

"We were talking about the town meeting actually," I say to Mum with a shrug.

"Yeah, well, you shouldn't be there," Ben says and stares at me. I see his hand move to his hair and roll my eyes.

"Here is your drink, Ben," I say ignoring his remark. I go back over to Tilly.

"Actually, April is my plus one and your dad has already said it's okay. I know you two have history but can you put it aside for one night?" Mum says to Ben.

"I've got no problem, Mrs Edwards," Ben says and turns to leave.

"Ben, you forgot your mince pie and I always tell you to call me Liz," Mum says, but the only thing left of Ben's presence is the flapping door.

Mum comes over with her cloth over her shoulder. "Are you okay?" she asks, looking me up and down.

"Yes Mum I'm a big girl, I can handle this," I say.

"And you still want to come to the meeting today?" she asks looking up at the wooden clock we have above the counter. It's only half one.

"April has to come to the meeting. It isn't like Ben owns the committee," Emily says, coming in with bags of shopping from the Co-op next door.

"Exactly, and we will be there too," Tilly says.

They envelope me in a hug but I am still nervous. Will he cause a fuss when he sees me later? I guess I will have to wait and find out.

CHAPTER 6

We pile into the committee room with the royal red carpet and chairs around a big wooden table.

"Darling, will you take the notes today?" Neil asks his wife and she gets out a notebook and pen.

"Welcome fellow villagers, old and new." Neil looks over his glasses and gives me a big smile. "Hello, April, how nice of you to join us this afternoon."

"Thank you Neil, urm, Mr Thomas. I can't wait to get involved in the Christmas events in the village," I say.

Maybe this won't be so bad. Ben and Paige are sitting across the room. I should stop watching them and focus on something else.

"Well, April, that is what we are here to discuss. The Christmas Fayre. Tilly, Ben, Paige, Naomi, Victor?" Neil looks between them. "Any news on setting the fayre up?"

"Yes, at the school we have had a few donations from the mums but no one has offered to have a stall," Tilly says.

"I could have a stall selling my cakes," I pipe up.

I notice Ben scoff and see him holding Paige's hand out of the corner of my eye. It shouldn't bother me as much as it does.

"So we have one volunteer for a stall and some donations. Come on villagers, what happened to the Christmas spirit? Can we organise the same people who did the bouncy castles for Birchlea-Heath Day to provide bouncy castles for this?" Neil asks around the room.

"Well, sir, we could but they said generally after November they don't provide bouncy castles due to health and safety," Naomi says.

"Keep asking them Naomi. We can come to some kind of arrangement, even if we have to have it inside the community centre," Neil says.

"I guess I can have a stall for my trinkets," Emily says. Her face blushes when everyone looks at her.

"Oh love, I am so proud of you," Mum says, squeezing her shoulders.

"I didn't know you still did that," I say to her.

"Yeah of course I do," Emily says and shrugs.

The door wafts open and in walks Mrs and Mr Corfoon, who was one of my old teachers. I can't believe they are here.

"Hello Dianne and Nigel, we are just organising the fayre," Neil says.

"Count me in for the hook a duck," she says and Neil writes it down.

"Ben?" Neil says, turning to his son sat two seats away from him. "Can you be Santa again?"

"Sure Dad," he says with a shrug. "I have to go back to work now though." He looks straight up at me and I feel his eyes burning through me. I look at Paige who is shaking her head looking confused. He isn't bothering me. I won't let him because I know he will crack before I do.

"Ben, I might actually need you, so can you come back here please?" Neil says.

Ben stays, sitting next to Paige again with his arms folded.

After Neil coerces a few more villagers into running stalls, we finally have the fayre sorted out. I make a mental note of the cakes and pies I want to make for my stall, feeling excited that I am getting involved.

"Our lovely nativity this year will be hosted by our very own year one and directed by Miss Tilly Walker and Roselyn, who can't be with us tonight as she had to rush home to her son. And next on the list we have our Christmas parade. I hate to have to inform everyone but it seems, from my notes from the council, there is no budget this year for our parade that we usually have going through the village," Neil says.

I hear whispers from around the table.

"Quiet everyone," Dawn says and everyone looks back at them.

"The council have informed us that, since the big C word they have had to make many budget cuts for events happening in and around our village and I'm afraid the parade is one of them. Mr Simon Miller himself has told us that we are more than welcome to organise it ourselves if we can. So do we have any volunteers?" Neil says.

You can literally hear a pin drop. I suddenly feel a lump in my throat and start spluttering.

"Ah, April, do you volunteer?" Neil asks. I bite my lip, not daring to look around. I can't exactly say no now, can I?

"Urm, sure Neil," I say. Mum hands me a plastic cup of water and I drink it.

"April can't do it on her own folks, anyone want to join in?" Neil looks around the room. "Son?" he asks Ben, who is staring into space. Is he even listening?

"What?" Ben asks, looking around at every pair of eyes on him.

"Were you not paying attention? Son, we need someone to volunteer to organise the parade and I am picking you for not listening," Neil says.

"Thanks Dad," Ben says sarcastically.

"Great, so that is sorted then. Ben and April, you are in charge of the parade this year," Neil says and I want to say something but he has already dismissed everyone.

Ben moves his blond curl out of his face and looks at me. I bite my lip. Oh god how did we end up organising the parade together?

◆ ◆ ◆

It's Friday, the day of the fayre. The rain hasn't stopped all night. Ben seems to be avoiding me which is all fine but we need to start talking about the parade, since we are working together. My stomach clenches thinking about it.

I serve my last cup of coffee while Emily and Tilly wait outside.

"Come on then," Tilly says when I go outside, and both of them link arms with me.

"You and Ben are the talk of the village, you know," Emily says.

"He won't even talk to me, I don't know how we are going to do this," I say.

"Well, the villagers are really excited that you two are organising the parade. You know, it's a huge deal," Tilly says.

"Yeah, talking about villagers, since when are you two friends? Didn't you hate each other at school?" I ask.

I'm feeling a bit like the third wheel as Emily and Tilly walk a little ahead of me. Have I really missed this much?

"We are friends. We were stupid kids that held grudges for no reason," Tilly says.

"Yeah, it was a long time ago," Emily says.

We reach the stalls and I start setting up mine. I was able to store my cakes and mince pies that I had baked for my stall in the fridge behind it.

I start setting up as the park fills with people. I see Ben and Paige in the Santa grotto. I desperately want to arrange a meeting between us but whenever he sees me he completely ignores me. Besides, right now I have a herd of children wanting mince pies.

"Need a hand?" Tilly asks.

"Please," I say and she comes behind the stall and helps me serve the queue that has built up.

When we have a few minutes, Tilly perches on the edge of a stool.

"I still can't believe you and Ben are doing the parade," she says.

"I know, I can't believe no one else asked to do it since they love it so much," I say.

"Yeah, people round here love it, but they don't want to put the effort in," Tilly says with a shrug.

"So, when did you become besties with my sister?" I ask, turning to her. I don't mean to sound accusing. Tilly's face flushes red and I raise my eyebrow at her.

"Urm, April, you remember when we used to play dares?" Tilly says and I watch her face as I nod slowly.

"Yeah," I urge her to carry on while the little stall is still quiet.

"Well, remember at one of our sleepovers you and Ben dared me and Emily to kiss?" she asks. She is fiddling with her hair and I want her to get to the point. It was a stupid game. We also ran down the streets but that I don't really want to remember that.

"Yes, Tilly, I still don't really know what you are getting at," I say.

I see a little queue gathering of villagers and I start to assist them with my homemade mince pies.

"Well, I'm gay," she stutters and, as a customer leaves, I turn around to her with my mouth gaping. "Are you really that surprised?"

"Urm, yes, I am," I say.

"I honestly thought you would have known from when we were younger," she says. She is biting her lip and I know she is nervous. Does she think I won't like her now?

"No, I had no idea Till," I say and I embrace her. "I'm so pleased you told me though."

"Is anyone serving here?" I hear a gruff voice say and we both turn around to face Ben. I swallow the lump in my throat.

"Yes," I say flustered. I smile at Tilly and walk over to Ben.

"What can I get you?" I say in my nicest voice. I know my smile is fake and I can't help it. A part of me mourns the friendship with Ben but words can't be taken back.

"I will take two mince pies and one chocolate Santa cupcake please," Ben says.

I bag them up for him and pass them over. Our hands brush and I can't ignore my skin standing up. I see him go to move his hair and hold my breath. What the hell just happened? I watch him walk out the door.

"Holy shit, the tension between you two," Tilly whispers the minute he's gone.

"I know. What are we going to do about the parade," I say.

"I will try to help out if I'm not working," Tilly says.

"It's all going to be a disaster. The whole village is expecting a beautiful Christmas parade how are we going to organise that?" I ask.

It feel like we've bitten off way more than we can chew and Ben hasn't even asked to discuss anything to do with it. It's going to be a disaster. We will be the talk of the village for years.

"I think it will be amazing, we will all help you. I will and Emily," she says.

The queues have died down. It must be the rain that has been threatening all day, which has finally unleashed. She leans against the stall.

"Talk about the devil and she appears," I say and smile to Emily. Emily does her tight smile.

"Till, shall we go?" she asks. I watch them walk away. A part of me feels jealous that I left and my friends and sister found other friends, but then I know I shouldn't be jealous. I should be happy.

I look around. I haven't had a customer for a while. Should I go and ask Ben if he wants to come to the stall to talk?

My phone starts vibrating and a text appears.

Meet me by the Santa's grotto

CHAPTER 7

I look around and no one is there. The other stalls are also empty. It seems we are finishing the fayre slightly early. I close my stall and lock it as I head across the field towards a giant tent decorated with stars. There's a small queue to see Santa and a few villagers seem to be dotted around at the hook a duck and shooting stall. The bouncy castle is already deflating.

"Ah, April, I am so pleased that you agreed to save our parade. Ben is just with some children right now, if you want to head in." Neil says lifts the tent and I head inside.

It's massive inside. Santa is sitting on his grotto throne, a giant red chair with gold on it, and there's a massive tree in the corner with gold and red tinsel hanging from the ceiling.

"You be a good girl for your daddy and I will ask my elves if they can make you a Baby Cry," the gruff voice says.

I raise an eyebrow as I stand in the corner. The little girl leaves without noticing me.

"I think you are a bit big to see Santa," Ben says dryly.

"Ben, did you message me?" I ask taking my phone out.

"No, my dad did," Ben says. "Look, Dad wants us to meet up to discuss the parade okay? I don't want to be friends, I don't feel anything for you any more just so you are clear, I have a girlfriend and I'm happy, but for some reason we are now in charge of this parade and I don't want to fail the rest of the villagers. So can you please work with me after this fayre? Can we meet at the coffee shop in about an hour?"

"But I don't have the keys for the coffee shop," I say.

"Yes you do. Hi love, hi Ben," Dad says, sneaking up behind me in an elf costume. Does everyone really care that much about the parade or are they trying to get me and Ben to be friends?

Dad hands me the keys and I look back to Ben.

"Okay, I will see you there," I say.

◆ ◆ ◆

I hang my coat up as I arrive at the coffee shop. It's strange being here so late and I watch the rain fall on the window from the dark sky. We only have about ten days to get a parade organised. I flick the coffee machine on and make Ben and myself a drink. I'm nervous. I sit and then I pace and I think about what Ben will say to me. He was fiddling with his hair when he was talking to me and that used to mean he was nervous. Does it still mean the same thing? Is all of this really a front because he is nervous I am back?

Ben appears in a brown coat and pulls down his fluffy hood. I put the coffee at the other end of the table I'm sitting at and wait for him.

He sits down opposite me and I bite my lip. Ben moves his hair out of his eyes and looks up at me. His hazel eyes that I used to think were so pretty. I still remember the hate in them when I left. It was as if they had turned to fire.

"Hi," I say. "I've made you a coffee. I don't know if you still like it black with one sugar."

He doesn't say anything. I get up to get my pad of paper and I can't help flicking the radio on just for background noise. I already feel tense. I don't know what to say to Ben and he is looking around as well, as if he wants to be anywhere else.

I come back with my pad and a pen.

"We need to make this the best parade of Birchlea-Heath. We need to make it magical for the children and adults and fun, too," I say.

"Yeah," Ben says so carelessly. His eyes are fixed on the table like it's the most interesting thing he's ever seen.

Is he doing this to get a rise out of me? My stomach

knots as I think about the villagers. We have to make this work. "I'm thinking we need Santa on a float. Maybe we could have some reindeer too with a sleigh as well," I say.

"Paige works at the wildlife centre. I'll see what she can do," Ben says.

"Great, we can have the local school on a float in nativity costumes," I say.

"We have sorted it out can I leave now?" Ben asks.

"Ben, look, I know we aren't best friends any more, but if we are doing this can you at least try to be interested for your village. For your mum and dad. Please," I say.

Our eyes meet and for a second I think maybe he has dropped his mood. Is he going to help with the details of the parade?

"Fine," he says as if it's the hardest word he has ever said.

"So you are Santa," I say and he nods. His eyes are still locked onto mine and my heart is flipping. I try to remind myself that Ben doesn't even like me let alone anything else and I need to concentrate on the parade.

"Don't you want a float for anything?" he asks.

"For what? I think we can both safely say that I'm not a good enough baker after all," I say.

He sighs and I wonder if this is it. Is he going to let

his guard down finally?

"Look, I'm sorry," he says, running his hands through his hair.

"Me too, I'm sorry you are still upset with me for leaving. And you were right, weren't you? This entire time you were right. My baking wasn't good enough," I say. I feel tears in my eyes. *Please don't cry.*

I look up at him and he swallows. The air feels tight and I don't know what he is going to say.

"Look, I didn't ask to be involved in this okay? So forgive me if I'm not exactly thrilled about it. And we both know you are good enough," he says.

"I also didn't ask for this," I say.

"Didn't you?" he asks, raising one perfectly groomed blond eyebrow and making my stomach do things it hasn't for years.

"No, I coughed and your dad volunteered me. Maybe your dad is trying to play cupid?" I say.

Ben makes an undignified scoff and I look away. "I don't think my Dad would do that. I've been with Paige for a year now."

"Well I don't know then," I say.

"Let's get on with this," he says, changing the subject before we start fighting again. I really feel like we might have turned a corner.

"Yes, let's," I say.

◆ ◆ ◆

I make us another drink. It's now almost midnight and we have only discussed the floats we might be using and what everyone might be able to do on them. I can't stop yawning.

"Should we call it a night?" he asks. He rubs his eyes and I feel like I'm going to fall asleep at this table.

"Yeah I guess so," I say yawning.

Ben gets up and I follow him. We walk home mostly in silence, our shoulders bumping every so often. When we reach my house, we are quite damp from the rain.

"I'll see you," I say and hover. I know he isn't about to hi five me but I don't know something shifted tonight and I think we both felt it. Ben hovers too before turning around and disappearing. I stand on my porch, wondering what I am feeling and why I'm feeling it. I can't feel things. I just can't.

CHAPTER 8

"So you actually met up last night?" Tilly asks.

It's midday the next day and we are having our lunch in Brew and Chill. I'm sitting at the table with Tilly and Emily.

"Oh god, were you alone?" Emily asks, raising her eyebrow.

"Yes, we spoke a little about what happened," I say.

"Wasn't he going to propose to you?" Tilly asks.

"You never told me that," Emily says, looking at me.

"I didn't get the chance because I ran away, didn't I?" I say, putting my head in my hands.

"Do you want to be friends?" Tilly asks.

"I want to be civil. I definitely wouldn't mind being friends but I don't feel anything for Ben. Maybe leaving was for the best," I say.

"I was proud of you when you went. I missed you like mad but you were getting yourself out there, making a mark for yourself in the world," Emily says.

"You were kicking the world's bum. Showing it who was the boss," Tilly says and they turn to each other, smiling. It's my turn to raise my eyebrow.

"So less about my tragic life and more about you two. I've bloody missed you both," I say and throw my arms around them. They join in the weird three-way hug and pull away after a minute.

"I've missed you," Tilly says. "But I am going to have to go to work." Tilly and Emily do this weird hug thing that lasts longer than it should and then Tilly waves to Emily as she leaves.

I put my hands on my hips.

"What's going on?" I say.

"I don't know what you mean?" Emily mumbles, going bright red.

"Excuse me, April, can we have service?" Dawn asks. She stands at the counter smiling with her woolly hat and coat on.

"Sorry," I say getting up. "We aren't finished," I say to Emily, who sinks down in her seat. What is going on with them?

"Hi, Mrs- I mean Dawn. What can I get you?" I ask politely.

Dawn puts her glasses back on her nose. "I would like a vanilla flat white please, but what I really want to know is how did yesterday go? Ben told me you met up for the parade and we are so proud you two are doing this for the town."

"Thank you," I say, getting the machine ready and pumping the syrup into the cup.

"We are getting there but I feel like we've bitten off more than we can chew."

I pass her the cup and she hands me money.

"A little tip from me lovey, don't think too much about it. We don't need a Macy's parade here in Birchlea-Heath, just a few floats to light up the children of the village. You were a child here, you know what you would have liked." She takes her drink off the counter and walks out.

I look after her and think about what I used to love about the parade. I would always love the music and the lights. It didn't even matter if Santa was in a rubbish chair or I knew it was my dad in the Santa suit. It's was the fact that this was our thing in our village and it was so exciting, hearing the music through the window and stepping outside to see a long float full of Christmas music and crowds with excited faces. There would be so many lights draped around with people dressed as different Christmas characters.

"Hello, earth to April?" Mum puts her hands in front of my face. "Emily, is she okay?"

"Not sure Mum, she just served Mrs Thomas and I

didn't hear what she said."

"April?" She clicks in front of my face making me blink and snap out of my day dream of the parade.

"Hi Mum," I say blinking into focus again.

"Hello, I wanted to ask you how the meeting went with Ben last night," Mum says.

"It went okay. We discussed a little bit of the parade," I say.

"Did you end up snogging?" Mum jokes.

"No. Ben doesn't like me much and anyway, he has a girlfriend. I really think I would have been better paired up with Tilly or Emily," I say.

"Ben just needs some time. I imagine you coming back has stirred up some feelings," Mum says.

It's my turn to scoff. "I don't think so. I just want be civil while we work together," I say.

"Mark my words you just give it time and while you are here. Go and whizz this around to your dad and take your break. I have Emily on hand, and then I want you here making more mince pies," Mum says.

I grab the drink for Dad and head out into the drizzly cold afternoon. It looks like it's already getting dark. I look at the garage wondering if Ben is working today.

Sighing I walk into the post office and the radio

is playing Slade. Dad is facing away from me, whistling the tune, and I put his coffee down on the counter.

"Hi Dad," I say. "I won't stop. I've just brought you a drink."

Dad turns around with a grin on his face. His now greying features light up.

"Hello, April love, how is everything going?" Dad asks.

"Everything is good Dad, it's the last day of November which means it's officially the run up to Christmas," I say and hug him. He's so warm and cuddly and I tear up. I missed all of this when I lived in my stupid little flat thinking I was the next Mary Berry.

"So it is, and I have got you something," Dad says, disappearing again before coming back with a little present.

"Dad, you didn't have to."

Dad holds up his hands. "It's nothing much."

I open it and it's a roll of sellotape. He chuckles at the look on my face.

"Thanks Dad," I say.

"You never know when you are going to need it," he says with a wink.

CHAPTER 9

It's night time and we all pile into the pub.

"What is everyone having?" Tilly asks. We find a seat at one of the booths.

"Beer," we all shout at the same time and laugh.

"Gosh I have missed you," Emily says, leaning her head on me.

"Right you lot, I have a special night for you all. As you know, it's our fortieth annual mistletoe event, so in about twenty minutes I want everyone taking part to register their name," Harry says.

"Ooh, you should join in," Emily says.

"You never know who might be there," Tilly says and I know who she's hinting at but Ben and I are only just starting to be civil with each other. My stomach churns and twists with worry. I still don't know how we will pull this off.

"I don't think so," I say, shaking my head and taking my beer.

"So what happened last night?" Till asks.

"We sat in silence for a lot of the time and then we actually spoke like adults and it felt a little better like a balloon deflating. We parted ways and I think we cleared the air a little," I say.

"Remember what they say when you are little: the boy who is mean to you actually fancies you," Tilly says.

"I had an awful time with Timmy when I was younger he just wouldn't leave me alone," Emily says.

"This is different though, neither of us want to go back there again," I say.

"Yeah he is pretty angry you left him," Emily says.

"But that means he cares, right?" Tilly says.

"Everyone who is joining in our mistletoe event come and sit on one of these chairs," Harry says.

Emily takes my hand and Tilly's and we sit down on the chairs.

"Dad, I don't want to do this," I hear Ben's voice saying.

"Hi Ben," Tilly says.

"Can I join in too?" Paige asks and we all shuffle up.

"This mistletoe event has been here for many years. You always join in," Dawn says.

"I just don't want to," Ben says.

"I want to join in," Paige says.

"So it's all sorted then," Tilly says.

Harry comes over with his microphone.

"Line up everyone. First of all, we are going to do the older folks of our town and if you have a problem with snogging the older folks in the village then step aside, because we will be doing you youngsters very soon. So if you are new to the village -welcome. We have a little game we like to play this time of the year called the mistletoe kiss and everyone lines up. We have a seat for the kissees and a blindfold for everyone. You have to guess who you have kissed. If you guess right you get a free pint," Harry says.

We move out of the way and sit in a booth while Ben's mum and dad embarrass him by full on snogging in front of everyone. We giggle while we watch Ben going red.

Ben's mum and dad win and get their free beer. I watch my own dad guess who my mum is and when he gets it wrong Mum leaves. Poor Dad.

Now it's our turn.

"Kissees sit here please," Harry says, instructing me, Tilly, Naomi, Victor, Paige and a couple of younger people I have never seen before to come and sit down.

"Why are you joining in?" Ben asks when I get up.

"Why not," I say, ignoring his tone.

"Everybody put a blindfold on," he says. "And make sure you don't talk to the kissees."

There's silence as we wait for everyone to put a blindfold on and then we sit back and wait.

"Kissers ready?" he shouts and they shout.

"Kissees ready," he asks and we cheer.

My first person is someone I don't know. When we kiss it's light and I have no idea who it is. They quickly move on.

My third person stumbles over to me. They put their hands on me and we kiss. The kiss sends butterflies fluttering in my stomach. I don't want to think who it is but I have a feeling I already know. I pull away and I feel like Ben also knows it's me. He hovers and I can feel his breath on my face. Oh god why did we kiss? Do I still feel things for Ben?

He eventually moves on and the game carries on. When the last people kiss, Harry speaks into the microphone.

"Number one please stand in front of the person you think is your man or woman," Harry says.

"I'm number one," I hear a voice. From their voice alone I can't tell who it is.

"Okay, next up is Ben Thomas. Will you please stand in front of the person you think is your girlfriend."

I feel a shadow over me. Was it really Ben? I know I thought it. Does he think I'm Paige?

"Remove your blindfolds," Harry says and we do. Ben and I are face to face and he doesn't look happy.

"She's not my girlfriend," Ben says angrily. Oh shit we are going to be back to stage one again aren't we?

I look over at Paige still blindfolded with a guy I don't know in front of her.

"Bad luck guys," Harry says and I go to sit down with Tilly and Emily.

"Last up we have our last two." I see a guy about our age standing in front of Paige.

"Kissee, do you know who this is?" Harry asks.

"I think I do, It's my ex-boyfriend, James," she says. They remove their masks and I look at Ben who is fuming. Uh-oh.

◆ ◆ ◆

I am happy when I make my way to Brew and Chill the next day. Nothing else happened last night but I can't stop thinking about the kiss I shared with Ben at the mistletoe event.

I open up the bakery. Shutting the door behind me, I hang my coat up while I flick switches and turn the heating on. It's a little frosty this morning and I can't wait for the place to warm up.

I spend the next hour kneading bread, rolling out dough, cutting out cute little Christmas biscuits and putting them in the oven.

When the time shows seven and the sun starts coming up, I flip the closed sign around and start cleaning the tables.

Mum comes in.

"So are you going to tell me what exactly happened with you yesterday?"

"Nothing really," I say. And it's the truth. Yes I kissed Ben, but I haven't seen him since and he isn't exactly my biggest fan right now.

"Hmm, that isn't what your face is showing," she says and I start decorating Christmas trees with delicate icing and sprinkles.

"My face says I had a nice evening out with my sister and friend last night. Oh and meeting Ben's new girlfriend, she's nice," I say.

"If you are sure. I just want to make sure you're happy. I know being back here has set you back and I don't want you to think any less of yourself," Mum says and I hug her. I am really pleased to be back here again, despite everything that happened at Milly's and between Ben and me.

CHAPTER 10

"Oh hi," Ben says when he comes into the coffee shop. It was a pretend kiss, just playing a game, so why do I feel butterflies again?

"Hi," I say. He has taken off his coat and is wearing jeans and a Christmassy green jumper that makes his eyes pop.

"So, urm, I don't know if you've heard but we have a little issue at the canal, half of the village are there now," Ben says.

"That's why it's gone quiet then." Mum suddenly appears from behind the counter. "Why don't you go there now with Ben try and help them out?" Mum winks at us and I ignore what she's implying, feeling my cheeks burn

"Do you need my help?" I ask Ben.

"If you wouldn't mind," Ben says looking straight at me. I ignore the swirling sensation in my stomach and follow him outside.

"Where's Paige today?" I ask. I know it's nothing to

do with me but I haven't seen her today.

"She's at work," he says like he doesn't want to say any more about it.

"So what's happened then?" I ask changing the subject back.

"Someone dumped an ice cream truck in the canal. The residents are fuming. Dad is on the phone to the council right now," Ben says.

"Oh," I say as we walk across the wet muddy field. My feet are sinking into the grass.

"I also wanted to see you, you know, to discuss the floats some more. I feel like we didn't get very far and now, well, now I'm not sure why we are so awkward," Ben stutters. He runs his hands through his hair.

"Of course we can discuss it properly. I think we need to think back to when we were children and how much we loved the floats and how they made us feel the magic of Christmas," I say.

Ben smiles and I wonder if our memories of the floats are the same as mine. Does he get a warm glow when he thinks about Christmas too?

"We can do that," he says and I feel that chill again. The tension is gone between us.

When we get closer to the canal, we notice the crowds of villagers. "What the heck is going on here?" I ask.

"I think they are trying to get the ice cream van out," Ben says.

I spot my dad tugging on a rope.

"Dad, you'll break your back," I say and he just laughs.

"I'm made of strong stuff, love, come and help us pull it out," he says.

Ben grabs the rope and I grab a little further in front, down the hill. Victor is holding near the bottom.

"Three, two, one, pull," Bernie from the newsagent says and we pull.

"Ben, get inside the ice cream van. If you can get it started we might be able to drive it back up." Dawn says. "But please, heaven forbid, be careful."

Ben walks down the hill and enters the ice cream van. Apart from having been out in the rain, it's looking pretty clean. He starts the engine and mud starts spraying all over us. But with some pulling and revving from Ben, we get the ice cream van on top of the hill.

Ben gets out when we are safely back on the field and starts laughing at me covered in mud.

"Well done that boy," Bernie says, giving him a pat on the back and then hovering around me.

"It's okay, you don't have to touch me," I say.

"April, we didn't come here for a mud bath," Ben says, mocking me.

He runs off and I chase him, eventually catching up to him and putting my muddy hands all over his face. He makes the mistake of turning around and we are so close it would be so easy to kiss him again. Do I want to kiss him? I shouldn't after the way he was before. Everything just feels so wrong and, well, we had our chance.

Even with this thought, I feel my face getting closer to his. My brain scrambling as I try to think about this rationally. No, my brain has turned into mush as my lips nearly press to his.

"April? Ben, ah there you are." Ben's mum must have followed us. We spring apart like we've been electrocuted. Shit, did we really almost kiss again? Do we tell Paige? It didn't happen did it? But would it have?

"Mum, urm, what do you need?" Ben asks, stuttering and stumbling. Ben's mum looks between us.

"Paige is on her lunch break and has been looking for you," she says. "I'm not interrupting anything, am I?"

"No, of course not. April and I need to go home and change," he says.

"Yes we do," I say and we walk together back to the village.

"There you are." Paige crosses the road to join us in the doorway of the garage.

"Yeah, we had an issue in the park but it's sorted now," Ben says.

"Yeah, I am going to go home and get changed," I say.

"Bye, April. Baby, I want you to meet my friend James," I hear as I cross back to the bakery.

Will he tell Paige what we almost did. What we probably would have done if Ben's mum hadn't found us? Because I know I would have kissed him. I'm not sure if Ben would have kissed me though.

◆ ◆ ◆

"Please come for a piss up and a carol singing sesh?" Tilly asks.

It's getting dark already and after thinking about almost kissing Ben all day, I am getting a bit of a headache. But tonight is our carol service and I know Tilly and Emily want me in their group. Should we invite Ben and Paige into our group as well? Would that be weird?

I flip over my festive dough of bread and knead it again, throwing it down on to the floury counter.

"It won't be the same without you sis," Emily says.

They pull faces and I sigh. "You won't give in, will you?" I ask.

"No, I think you should give that poor bread a rest as well. You were really giving it some welly," Tilly says.

"Yeah you were like Rocky, which makes me think you have seen a certain person today and I want to know everything," Emily says.

I take my apron off and wash my hands, getting ready to go out. I slip a painkiller into my mouth, knocking it back with a cup of water, and hope for the best. I'm not exactly dressed the best for carolling. I know it's our tradition but I can't really be bothered to go. I would prefer to relax and have a bath.

CHAPTER 11

I tell the girls what happened along the way.

"I can't believe you nearly kissed him again," Emily says.

"I know, but the thing is he has Paige," I say

"Yeah I know. But Paige has been spending a lot of time with James," Tilly says.

"Who is James?" I ask.

"Oh, I don't know, I think they used to be friends," Emily says.

"No, they are exes," Tilly says.

We both look at her.

"How do you know?" I ask.

"Paige told everyone at the mistletoe kiss," she says.

We are silent for a minute.

"Back to you and Ben though, do you like like him?" Emily asks.

"I shouldn't after the way he was when I first got

here," I say with a sigh. I wish I hadn't told them. I hope no one overhears us either.

"Well, you've got it all out, all of the feelings you both had and well-that could be it," Tilly says.

We open the door to the pub, already brimming with locals. I see Ben's mum and dad sitting at one of the tables. Ben and Paige are with them with their backs to us.

The festive celebrations have already started by the looks of it. Victor is up singing the karaoke version of 'Merry Christmas Everybody' at a deafening volume while spilling his pint of beer all down him.

We make our way to the bar.

"What you having?" Tilly asks.

"I'll pay," Emily says.

"No, I will. You paid last time," Tilly says.

"Last time?" I ask, waving to Harry.

"Yes, we do have a social life without you," Tilly says.

Emily just looks down at the ground.

"What we having girls?" I ask.

"Ooh, we should get some Sourz. It will be just like before you went," Tilly says.

I laugh. "But they were horrible."

"Yeah they were," Emily agrees with me.

"Okay then, boring OAPs let's do shots then," Tilly says.

"We've actually started our spicy Christmas shots if you want to try them," Harry says.

"Ooh spicy," Tilly says.

"Hello guys," Paige says coming over and sitting next to Tilly and Emily in a booth. Ben sits next to me. "It's so nice to finally get some time with Ben's friends and the famous April."

"Yeah here she is in the flesh," Tilly says.

"I've heard so much about you. I was actually a little intimidated because Ben talks about you so much," Paige says.

I look to Ben who shrugs. What has he been saying about me?

"Your drinks guys," Harry says, bringing them over on a tray.

"Bloody hell woman, how many did you get?" Emily asks, eyeing up the tray. There are at least ten shot glasses all glittery and a different shade of red.

"I wanted us to have a choice," Tilly says.

"Oh, guys. I want you to meet James," Paige says waving him over.

"Hi everyone," James says shaking all of ours

hands.

James has dark blond hair, he has a small beard made up of wild wiry hair and is dressed in the brightest jumper I have ever seen. His fingers have many rings on them.

"Do you want to join us?" Tilly asks him.

"Nah, I don't drink. I like to keep my soul clean. Alcohol is bad for you," James says.

"Fair enough, more for us," I say.

"To us," Emily says and we hold up the shots and drink them. Oh god it's awful but I feel the alcohol warming me up.

"Are you coming carolling with us?" I ask Paige.

"Yeah, I would love to. Is that okay babe?" Paige asks Ben.

"Yeah, sure. April, I was hoping that we can discuss the floats tonight," he says.

"Or you could discuss something else," Tilly says under her breath. I kick her under the table and ignore Ben messing with his hair. Paige hasn't noticed.

"Great, is it okay if James joins us? He is back in town to look after his granddad and he doesn't know anyone," Paige says.

"Of course, the more the merrier," Tilly says.

"Fab," Paige says.

"I'm going to go and check on my granddad," James says.

"I'll come with you," Paige says.

We watch them leave and turn to Ben.

"What?" he asks.

"They look cosy," Emily says, downing another shot.

"Yeah they do, they look good together," Tilly says.

"Yeah, well it isn't like that," Ben says.

"Come on guys, leave it off," I say, trying to keep the peace.

"We are going to get ready to go," Emily says, pulling Tilly with her.

"So what is it you want to talk about?" I ask.

"I thought the ice cream van could be used at the parade," he says.

I nod. "We could make it a Christmassy ice cream float and stop every so often for the children to get ice cream."

"Exactly," he says. "I also thought, since we are arranging this together, that you would want to come to the sanctuary Paige works at to meet the reindeer."

"Sounds great Ben, I would love to," I say.

"You two aren't snogging again are you?" Tilly says

THE MOBILE BAKERY AT THE CHRISTMAS PARADE

coming back with our hymn book. I didn't notice before that we are leaning so close to each other. I can smell his aftershave and it's beautiful.

"Hello everyone and welcome to our Christmas boogie. Warm up before you all head outside to sing your hearts off. Can I firstly have all the lovers here for this first Christmas song," Harry says into a microphone that starts beeping loudly after he finishes speaking, then the Ed Sheeran Christmas song comes on. Couples rush to the dance floor. Tilly and Emily go to dance too.

"Do you want to dance babe?" Paige asks.

"Yes," Ben says. They go off to dance. I watch Tilly and Emily and Ben and Paige and feel a stab of something. I want this too.

"Fancy a dance? I have to warn you I am not the best, but hey-ho," James says.

"Okay," I say.

I don't want to dance with him but I watch Ben and Paige over James' shoulder. James is tripping over my feet.

"Ow," I say and pull away.
"I told you I can't dance," he says.

James lets go of me and disturbs Paige and Ben.

"You've been left too?" I ask as Ben joins me. He downs a shot and hands me one.

"Yeah, turns out I have. But maybe we can dance?

You know, as friends," he says quickly.

"Yes," I say and he takes my hand, leading me to the middle of the floor. Is this my chance to ask about what he has been saying to Paige?

I lean my head on Ben, breathing in his scent. He smells amazing and he has clearly made an effort to look nice tonight. Why does this feel so right but obviously so wrong? I can't help sighing as he spins me around and pulls me to him. The swirling in my stomach returns. In my head I am screaming that he has a girlfriend, but the shots and my feelings are getting in the way.

I make the mistake of looking up at Ben and the direct eye contact makes me feel like electric pulses are shooting through me.

"Ben... I," I whisper, not knowing really what I want to say.

"Don't," he whispers back into my ear. I turn and our noses brush.

"I'm not...I... don't know what to think of any of this," I say.

My heart is hoping I kiss Ben again and we talk about all of this. We really should talk about it. All of the hurt we felt before. Everything we felt when we split up. It's been building and I feel like this isn't helping at all.

Ben pulls away. "We can't do this," he says. "Do you want to go carolling now? I think I need the fresh air."

I nod.

"I'm going to ask the others if they are ready to go," he says.

I wait by the door.

"Are you going carolling together?" she asks.

Emily and Tilly, and James and Paige head over with Ben.

"Remember you need to split into groups of three," Mum says.

"Okay, I will go with Ben and April," Paige says.

James doesn't look sure.

"Come on, you will be okay with us," Tilly says.

"We're taking the houses on Slater Street," I say.

"Have fun," she sings. I think she's enjoying this.

"I am so excited you guys," Paige says, putting her arm around us.

"Me too. It's nice for my friends to spend time with my girlfriend," Ben says. They kiss and I don't know why but it stabs me a little. At least it's not raining any more.

"Of course, and I can't wait to see your reindeer tomorrow," I say.

"Yes, every year your cute little village visits my sanctuary and I get to be involved again. This year

I can't wait to be on the float with Ben," she says.

"I can't wait as well," Ben says and they kiss. Oh god, I am going to be a third wheel aren't I?

"Well we still need to talk about the floats," I say.

"I know we do and we will make time for that," Ben says.

We make our way down the hill toward the coffee shop and I wonder if we will get to talk about what happened when we nearly kissed

I nod. "We need to talk about other things too."

"I know," he says.

"Like what have you been saying about me," I start. "And sorry for everything I said that night."

"You don't have to do that," Ben says. "It doesn't matter." He ignores my first question but I can't help the feeling in my chest.

"Come on you two, you have plenty of time to catch up," Paige says, pulling our arms to the first house on the street.

I'm not a huge singer. Paige surprisingly is and just belts out the entire song like it's her job and I am impressed. I even look at Ben, who is looking in awe of her. We finish 'O Come Let Us Adore Him' and the neighbours give us sweets.

We slowly move across the road. Paige takes the lead and we just sway in the background. Weirdly,

Ben squeezes my hand while we sing. It makes my heart jump.

We reach the last house on the street and I am so tired. My feet are also hurting. I yawn involuntarily. My feet are so cold I can't feel them any more and I want nothing better than to go to bed. *But not with Ben.*

"Ready guys?" Paige asks. My heart flips.

"Yes," we say.

The door opens and we start singing. My teeth chatter and I am pleased Paige is louder than both of us. The neighbour offers us a mince pie before we leave.

"I feel like Jack on the Titanic," Ben says shivering.

"Really? I don't think it's too bad," Paige says.

"I second that. I am so cold," I say.

"Do you want my gloves for a bit?" Ben asks.

"Yes please." He gives me his gloves and I slip them on. They are so warm from being on his hands and I can't control the butterflies in my stomach.

"This has been really fun, but Ben babe, I think we should head home," Paige says.

"Yeah, of course." Ben says. Paige is already walking and we follow her slowly. "I just want to say I hated that you were back when you first came back but now I'm glad you are here."

"Me too, I was so nervous to see you again," I say.

"We will see you tomorrow, April," Paige says as we catch up with her. She throws her arms around me. I almost stumble backwards.

"See you tomorrow," I say and walk home. My heart is thumping. Oh god, I am in love with Ben, again.

CHAPTER 12

It's not surprising that I have woken up in an almighty Christmas mood. The only thing that's stops me being fully there is I can't be with Ben because he has a girlfriend. I'm trying to think about my friendship, because if I think of us being anything more it hurts too much. I make my way to the coffee shop and it isn't even five yet.

I flick classic Christmas songs onto YouTube on my phone and when 'Merry Christmas' comes on again I think about what happened yesterday. I actually kissed Ben and it felt amazing. It makes me feel giddy inside like I am still that eighteen-year-old with no responsibilities and not someone who has just moved back home because her career has failed.

I look around at the coffee shop as my shortbread bakes in the oven and my mood dips a little. I should be thankful I still have a job. But I should be a superstar baker by now. I should have been one of the people who still had their jobs at Milly's. I had been there my entire adult life. Baking is all I have ever known. It's pretty much all I'm good at. I don't really know what I want to do now. I smile thinking about Ben saying I am a good baker. If only I won the lottery though and then I could own my own bakery with my name on it. I could open it nearer to mum.

I'm thinking of names I could call my bakery when Emily comes through the door.

"What the fuck happened to you?" I ask. Her usual blonde hair is matted and she looks terrible.

"I slept over at Tilly's," she mumbles, getting away from me.

"Really?" I ask. Her face is bright red. "Did anything happen?"

She doesn't answer me. Does this mean that Emily could be gay too?

"So what's going on?" I ask.

"I don't know." She sits down with her head in her hands. "I don't know what it means Ape, I don't know anything and I am so confused."

"You sound like me," I say and she laughs.

"Yes, but your love life is less complicated. I have spent my entire life denying who I am," Emily says.

"Not really though I have reconnected with Ben and it's brought up feelings I don't want," I say.

"Really, you have feelings for Ben?" she asks.

"And you have feelings for Tilly?" I ask.

"Yes, but what will Mum and Dad think?" she asks.

"They aren't going to disown you for being you. If Tilly makes you happy then they should be happy," I say.

"So are you going to tell me what happened when you went carolling?" Emily asks.

"Nothing happened. Ben and I have decided to be friends," I say.

I take the shortbread out and leave them to cool down.

"That never happens when there are feelings," she says. She gets up, following me.

I sigh. When we were younger, we used to talk about boys and all sorts. When did we become so secretive about our lives? She didn't want to tell me what has been going on with her. She didn't even come out to me. I had to put the pieces together, and I am reluctant to tell her about Ben.

"Ape?" she says. "You don't have to lie to me."

"Okay, I have no idea what is going on between us," I say. "And it isn't like anything can is it? Being friends is as close as I will get and I should be grateful because at least he doesn't hate me, but then we kissed and everything just felt perfect."

"So you would want to be more if Paige wasn't around?" she asks.

"Is that a horrible thing to want?" I ask.

My head is so confused and saying it out loud makes me sound horrible. Of course I don't want to get rid of Paige. Annoyingly she is lovely and I can see why he likes her. But how can we organise the parade when there's feelings?

"Maybe just see what happens. Yes he has a girlfriend now, but what if she isn't the one?" Emily says

"How can she not be?" I say.

I get out the piping bags and make up four batches of icing in Christmassy reds, greens and ice blue and hand her one of them. Emily is known for her eye for fine details that's why she makes little crafts and sells them on Etsy. I take the icy blue and make some snowflake lines on them and then sprinkle edible glitter on them. When we are finished, we stand back and look at our creations.

"I've missed talking about boys and well, girls, with you, and baking…no actually, more so the baking than anything. I've missed having my big sister with me," Emily says.

"I'm not going anywhere again," I say, feeling like I should never have left.

"So you aren't ditching us again?" Emily asks.

"No way," I say. We hug and I know I made the right decision. Even if nothing happens with Ben ever, at least I have my friends and family here.

THE MOBILE BAKERY AT THE CHRISTMAS PARADE

❖ ❖ ❖

"Ready to go?" Ben walks in with his coat all zipped up and a hat and gloves on. He lets the cold in from the door.

"Ready," I say, getting my own coat on. I don't know why I feel really excited to be going out in the car with Ben but I do.

"Good luck," Mum says.

"Take a coffee each and a snowflake." Emily slots two shortbread snowflakes into a paper bag and gives them to me.

"Hang on let me get one for Paige," I say, ignoring the eyebrow raise from Emily.

I walk out to the car park behind the coffee shop. Ben opens the door for me and then gets in next to me. I'm not sure if I should be feeling as excited as I am being next to him but, like Emily says, we should see how it goes.

"It's freezing in here," I say, blowing out my breath in a cloud of steam. "Hang on, where's Paige?"

"Let me put the heating on for you. Paige is working today. She's waiting for us. Put the radio on if you want to," he says, flicking switches in the car and then starting it up.

I fiddle with the dial until 'Santa Tell Me' comes on and I sit back happy.

I look out the window as we drive away from the coffee shop. The ice cream truck is in the garage.

"Ben, what's going on with the ice cream van?" I ask.

"I did a MOT test on it and it seems to be working, I contacted the council and they basically said it's our property to get rid of," he says. "Why?"

"I was just wondering," I say. "Do you think we can actually serve ice cream in it at the parade?" I ask.

"Yes. I'm not entirely sure who would serving the ice cream, or if anyone would want it in December, but we can figure that out," Ben says.

"I was thinking of asking Mum if she wants to share a float and we can have baking and Christmas drinks together," I say.

"If you like, unless your mum wants to serve drinks in the ice cream van, or you could make cakes in there," Ben says.

I feel my body tingling with excitement. Could this be it? I can't afford to have my own cake shop but I could run a cake stall for events.

"You're quiet, are you okay?" he asks and reaches a hand over to me. He squeezes my hand and I smile.

"Do you think I could use the ice cream van as a cake stall? If you're okay with it?" I ask him.

"You've always dreams of having your own bakery. Would you be satisfied with the ice cream van?" he asks.

"I think so," I say excitedly. I want to throw my arms around him but last time we did that we kissed.

"Then take it. The council aren't interested. I could help you make it look a bit nicer. You know I've always liked painting. I just never pursued it," Ben says.

"I remember your GCSE art, it was amazing," I say and smile as the radio changes to 'One More Sleep.'

"I'll help decorate the other floats too," Ben says.

"Yes, and yes of course I think you should decorate the ice cream van," I say.

I smile in my seat, looking over at Ben and his eyes are twinkly like he's rediscovered what he has always wanted to do. I feel the same. I desperately want to open a bakery but I've never had the money to do it. Maybe after the parade I can carry on selling cakes.

"Thank you April, for believing in me," Ben says and smiles at me.

"You are welcome," I say.

I get all tingly again when we get drive into the car park and Ben's hand is touching mine. He stops the car and we get out and make our way up the dirt path.

"I can't wait to meet the reindeer," I say.

"Me too, it will be absolutely perfect .Paige looks after them with her mum and dad," Ben says.

I nod. Maybe we can pull this off and make the best parade ever for the villagers. Then I can stop feeling guilty for leaving.

"Yes, it will. Ben, I can't wait to see them," I say.

"Me too, and I am sorry for being a jerk the other day," he says

"That's okay, I'm sorry too. I said those things out of spite and now I'm back, I'm really enjoying spending time with you," I say.

Before he can answer, Paige appears at the fence with a huge grin on her face. "I'm so pleased you are here," Paige says and hugs both of us. "Follow me."

CHAPTER 13

We follow her into the staff area and sit down on the comfy sofas.

"So I would advise that we don't use the reindeer on the parade float, you know, after last year," Paige says.

"What happened last year?" I ask, looking from Ben to Paige.

"One of the reindeer got scared and jumped off the float. No one got hurt luckily, but it definitely disrupted everything," Paige says.

"Yeah, we don't want that. Maybe we can have a pen in the park where the children can meet the reindeer," I say.

"Sounds great," Paige says and she smiles at both of us. Ben takes her hand and I feel like a third wheel. "Is there any chance before the children pet the reindeer, then maybe we can ask for donations to cover food and drink. They will need food and drink throughout the day, and shelter if it's freezing."

"It was a big success last year," Ben says.

"Hopefully it will be again this year," I say.

"So what is the date you need them on?" Paige asks.

"The fifteenth of December?" Ben asks me.

"Yes," I say. Though that's only two weeks away. Can we really pull this off?

"Great, I will bring the reindeer while the parade is moving, so baby you will have to do the float on your own," Paige says.

"That's okay. I'll miss you though," Ben says.

"I'll miss you more," she says and they start snogging.

"Okay, we'll start the parade at midday, so if you can maybe bring them then," I say. They aren't listening to me.

I wait for them. Eventually they stop and look at me.

"I'm sorry April. What were you saying?" Paige asks.

"I said we are starting at midday, so can you bring the reindeer then?"

"Of course, would you like to meet them?" she asks.

"Yes," I say.

Ben and Paige hold hands while we walk and I

wish I had stayed in the car. I just can't get my head around these new feelings that I don't enjoy having.

We finally stop at a stable.

"So we have nine reindeer, just like Santa. We don't give them names because we like the children who visit us to think they are Santa's reindeer," she says.

"Hi," I say, putting my hand out to the reindeer nervously.

"They are friendly, you can pet them," Paige says encouragingly and I do. The reindeer's fur is warm. Their antlers are like tree branches.

"What do you think, Ape?" Ben asks.

"Perfect," I say.

"Great," Paige says.

The conversation is clearly over and the way they are looking around makes me think they want to be alone.

"Do you want me to wait in the car?" I ask. I wait until I am away from them before the tears come.

❖ ❖ ❖

I flick the radio and the first bells of 'All I want for Christmas is You' come on. How ironic. All I want for Christmas is Ben but how can I say anything when he looks so happy?

Ben comes back a little while later and we head back to Brew and Chill. My phone starts buzzing.

"It's Tilly," I say. Ben turns the radio down.

"Hi Till," I say.

"April, where are you?" Tilly's voice comes through the phone. I put it on speaker.

"I'm in the car with Ben," I say.

"Hi Till," Ben says to the phone.

"Okay, I won't ask until later but I really need a favour, if you could both stop by the school," Tilly says.

"What do you need help with?" I ask. I daren't look at Ben.

"So we are doing our nativity in a week and we need painters to paint sets. I wouldn't ask if I wasn't desperate," Tilly says.

I finally look over at Ben. Does Ben want to do this? Would he want to paint the set with me? He will be kind of doing his dream job.

"Yes," Ben answers. He smiles over at me. I feel that feeling again. I wish I didn't feel it but I do.

"It's a yes from us Till," I say.

When we disconnect the phone I look over at him.

"Ben, why didn't you follow your dreams if you wanted to be an artist or painter?" I ask.

"Because being an artist or even a painter doesn't pay the bills, does it? When you left, I was eighteen. I was still at my first job and then old Harry died and I took over the garage, since his son didn't want anything to do with it," Ben says.

"Oh Ben, that's so sad," I say. We have arrived in the car park at the school and all I can think about is me leaving him. The guilt from it still eats away at me.

"It is what it is." He shrugs.

"But it doesn't have to be. Is it just you at the garage?" I ask.

"Don't worry about me. I thought I had the worse luck ever, but actually the garage is where I met Paige so it isn't all bad," Ben says and gets out of the car. I follow him into the school.

"I'm so pleased to see you both." Tilly hugs both of us as we walk into the reception area of the school.

"We are happy to help," I say.

"Of course, anything is better than boring paperwork." Ben shrugs. He always seemed so dedicated to his job when we were younger.

"Well, I need inns painted please and the night sky. Emily is already there so just grab some paint and get cracking," Tilly says and leaves us to it.

"Ma'am yes ma'am." Ben salutes behind Tilly's back and I giggle.

We walk into the hall and Emily is sitting on the stage with a huge inn made from cardboard, which has a back on it so it stands up.

"I'll tackle the sky if you want to do another inn," Ben whispers so we don't disturb anyone. Victor and Bernie are already painting in one of the corners while quietly talking, so I grab a blank inn and sit on the step of the stage with my brush.

"Want a bit of company?" Emily asks, bringing her inn closer. "I have to say this looks very cosy."

Ben hasn't heard her. Thank god.

"Not at all. How are you?" I ask.

"Good," Emily answers without looking at me.

"Em?" I ask, stopping painting for a second.

"Okay, I am so confused. I asked Tilly what we are? and she basically said having fun, but what if I don't want to just have fun? And then I'm thinking all of these things like she doesn't want to tell anyone about us, which I get, I haven't even told Mum and Dad, so I get it," she says.

"Oh Emily, I'm sorry. I can be there when you tell Mum and Dad if you want. I think you need another conversation though, to set the boundaries -because if she wants fun and you want more, you can't keep going on like that. You'll only get hurt," I say.

"And you need to take your own advice," Emily says.

"I know but it's different with me," I say. We laugh because it's ridiculous.

"Part of me wants to carry on regardless, because at least we are sort of together but not officially, and part of me wants it to be completely official. But at least Tilly isn't with someone else," Emily says. She finishes her door and puts it to dry.

Before I can answer, Ben comes over to me with his finished sky.

"I'll talk to you in a bit," Emily whispers and leaves us to it.

"Hey," Ben says and sits next to me, putting his sky next to my door.

"Oh, hi," I say.

"So I wanted to talk to you about something," he says and puts a bit of paint onto my cheek.

I laugh and slap his hand away.

Ben's phone interrupts the moment and he pulls it out of his pocket.

"It's Paige," he says.

"Oh," I say looking away.

"I want to ask her to marry me," Ben blurts out.

Right then I feel like my gut is being squeezed. Tears well in my eyes and I need to get away.

"Oh right," I say. I don't want my voice to betray me. I shouldn't be disappointed. He has a girlfriend who he wants to marry. But then what about me? Did he feel anything the other day when we kissed? Because I thought something was there. Was there something there or did I imagine it?

"I'm not really sure why I told you. Is it inappropriate?" he asks, mumbling.

I desperately want to ask him about the other night but it feels so wrong now. I'm too late because he wants to marry Paige.

"Of course it isn't," I say. My voice is wobbling all over the place. I look around the room for Emily but she looks busy painting with Victor and Berni. *Leave him alone. Just go home.*

"Great, because she is amazing and well... I don't know, I just didn't want things to be weird," he says moving his hair from his face again. He's nervous. Is he nervous of my reaction?

"Nothing is weird, I'm completely fine. But I should probably go though, I need to get back to the coffee shop," I say.

I practically run away before Ben can say anything and wait until I'm well out of the car park and into the drizzly rain before letting the tears fall.

CHAPTER 14

It's a few days after I ran out on Ben and I have been conveniently avoiding him while killing myself thinking about him with Paige. The tears fall again as I knead the dough. Why have I let myself be put in this situation? Why did we have to kiss? I think I preferred it when he hated me.

I've stayed completely focussed on my work for now and not had a second thought about the parade until tonight. Neil wanted to do a catch up meeting with the town so I can't say I won't go.

At six am, I turn the sign to open and take some apple muffins out of the oven leaving them to cool down before putting my batch of mince pies in to cook.

I make myself a drink, leaving the money in the till, and sit down.

"Morning Ape, how are you?" Emily comes in, taking her coat off and coming over. When I don't answer she asks, "Are you okay?"

"Sort of," I say. I wonder if she heard what happened.

"Okay, spill," she says.

I tell her what happened after she left and she sighs. "You were too late."

"Yeah, I really thought something happened the other night, but they are serious Em, he wants to propose," I say. I feel the tears coming again.

"I'm sorry Ape, but you were away for years. He couldn't wait for you forever," she says.

"I feel like an absolute fool. I didn't expect him to wait for me but marriage Em, it's a huge deal. And now we have a meeting at eight this morning and I have to sit with him. I walked out yesterday when he said he wanted to propose," I say, putting my hands over my face.

"Morning," Tilly says and sees me.

"Morning," I say, less than enthusiastic.

"I heard what happened," she says.

"Does the whole school know?" I ask and she shakes her head.

"I'm sorry for asking both of you to paint but we were desperate," Tilly says.

"No, I am glad I did and I'm glad he did too. I didn't know he actually wanted to pursue painting and he just ended up at the garage because it was a job,"

I say.

"I didn't know it either. He looked happy there to me," Emily says.

I leave them at the table while I put the muffins on the shelf, change the sign and price and then take the mince pies out of the oven and onto the cooling rack.

"Okay, I've got to go, we are doing nativity practice," she says.

I watch as she hovers around Emily and they do a weird hug thing before a peck on the cheek.

I clean my area, giving them privacy.

"I'm so damn frustrated," Emily says

"So you haven't told her you want a relationship yet?" I ask.

"No, and every day it kills me more," she says.

"Well, what I just watched is embarrassing," I say and she rolls her eyes. I freeze hearing the song on the radio. Oh god.

"What?" Emily looks at me.

"It's the song Ben and I danced to and the one we kissed to," I whisper. The song sends shivers down my spine and a tingle in my stomach. I wish I told him right there how I feel.

"Oh god, Apc." She comes over and hugs me.

"What if this is it? What if they do get married and

have children and I have to live in the same village and see them every day. How can I live with it for the rest of my life? I could have said something but I didn't," I say between sniffles.

"He hasn't asked her yet so they aren't even engaged yet. And if they do, oh well, you will find someone else and you won't care about them," Emily says. She strokes my head.

The door flings open and Mum walks in. "What's going on?" she asks and I pull away from Emily.

"Ben wants to marry Paige," Emily says.

"Oh. And how do you feel about that?" Mum asks.

"I missed my chance, Mum," I say.

"Oh love. I'm sorry," she says and hugs me. I smell her perfume and smile. She used to wear this perfume when I was a child and it just brings back memories.

"Well you know what I'm going to say, don't you?" she says pulling back from me.

"That I shouldn't waste my time chasing one man," I say.

"Exactly, now I have heard there is a new boy in the village called James. Why don't you ask him for a drink?" Mum says. "He will be at the meeting. speaking of, we have to get going now," she says.

We say goodbye to Emily, who has agreed to watch the coffee shop while we attend the meeting.

THE MOBILE BAKERY AT THE CHRISTMAS PARADE

I stare out of the window as mum listens to Christmas music on the radio. We pull up at the community centre and everyone is waiting.

"Morning April," Dawn says. I look around the car park and we are all waiting for Neil to open the doors.

"Morning, what's going on?" I ask.

"Oh, don't mind Mr Thomas, he's just getting his meeting diary out. He forgot it so he had to go all the way home. Silly bugger," she says rolling her eyes.

"I'm here now, sorry," Neil says, clutching his diary. I look around and Ben isn't here.

"Is Ben not coming?" I ask.

"Yes he is love, he's just having a breakfast date with Paige, lovely girl she is," Dawn says.

I feel wobbly. My legs are wobbly, stomach feels wobbly, and I feel like I might collapse. Is he proposing to her right now? Would she say yes if he did? I shake the thought away.

"Don't worry though, he told me to tell you he will be back mid-meeting. He wants to start painting the floats," Dawn says.

I follow everyone into the hall feeling numb. I want to go home. I want to get into my bed and say the parade is off. I don't want to do it any more. Ben still isn't here but I see James. He waves to me.

"Hello everyone, meeting commences at one minute past eight," Neil says.

"My most important question today is directed to you, April. I want to know what is going on with the parade," he says.

I really wish Ben was here. I'm not in the right mood for all the eyes on me right now. Why did I agree to this?

"Urm, Neil, we've made some progress. That ice cream van we have found is being used in the parade for my cakes. We are going to paint it up and I am going to bake cakes for the parade. We have the reindeer for the entire day on the fifteenth of December and yes, they will be at the park in a pen and not on a float. Talking of floats, today we are getting them ready to paint and decorate too," I say.

Everyone is looking at me and my face is bright red. My heart is racing and I am fiddling with my hands.

"That's great April, after last year's disaster I think this is for the best," Neil says. "So I wanted to ask about music. Have you got a band booked for the stage?"

"Urm, no not yet," I say. I write it down in my phone in my to-do list.

"I'm sorry Mr -Neil can I interrupt? I just want to say that I have a band and I would be happy to play at the parade," James says.

I look over at him, my mouth wide open.

"April and James, you can discuss this and get back to me, yes?" Neil asks.

The rest of the meeting is incredibly boring. Mrs Darcy complains that the howling from the 'wild animals' needs looking at and Victor complains about the bins being emptied.

"Meeting dismissed," Neil says and I stand up, feeling relieved, and push my way through everyone to stand outside. It must be zero or close to and as I breathe my nose stings and my eyes water. I let the tears come as I walk up to the ice cream van and see a piece of paper attached to it.

I'm so sorry I'm not back yet but if you want to start painting go ahead! I will see you soon ✶ *Ben*

The x is crossed out and it just says Ben. Did he think it meant something if he left the kiss there? Does he know that I feel something for him now? I sigh and take my coat off, feeling the icy wind getting to me. I could get started on the painting I suppose.

"Ah April, I want to let you know we have paint in our church reception for you to use. Just help yourself," Neil says. I nod and we walk through the church.

"April, do you want some help with the painting?" James asks.

"Sure," I say. We see my mum and she gestures for me to come over.

"Are you coming back to the coffee shop?" Mum asks. She sees James and raises her eyebrow.

"I'm going to start painting and James is helping," I say. "Is that okay?"

"Yes it's okay, but be back by midday, Emily needs a break," she says and leaves.

We bring the buckets of paint out into the car park and remove the lids.

I look over at James and he smiles at me. This isn't too bad and it takes my mind off of Ben proposing to Paige at least.

"James I was thinking would you like to go out for a drink?" I ask.

"Sure that sounds good. Now, what colour are you thinking?" James asks.

"Well it can't look too Christmassy, otherwise I won't be able to use it for the rest of the year," I say.

"How about this purple?" he asks and I nod. It's a gorgeous colour.

James tips it into a paint tray and I hear the crunch of footsteps and whispering.

"Oh, April, you decided to stay and paint," Ben says. I look up and see him with his arm around Paige and something twists in my gut.

CHAPTER 15

"Hi guys," I say to Paige and Ben, trying to be upbeat and happy but at the same time feeling like my heart has been crushed.

"Need some help?" he asks.

"If you like," I say non-committally. Of course I want him to help me. I am so angry with myself for having all of these feelings just swirling around me. How do I deal with them?

"Okay," he says coming over.

"Can I help too?" Paige asks. I nod and they both grab a paintbrush.

"Come and work with me babe," Ben says.

"I'm just going to wash my hands," James says.

"Okay," I say. I want to ask if they are engaged yet. Why haven't they mentioned anything? Did it not happen? And why does that make me so happy?

Ben's mum comes over while we are painting. "I'm so pleased you are getting involved Paige. It's nice to see the village working together," Dawn says.

"Thanks Mum. I wanted to let you and Dad know the floats are on their way so we can start decorating them soon," Ben says.

"And James is playing at the park at the parade," I tell Ben's Mum.

"Of course he is," I hear Ben muttering. I look over at them both but he is still painting. Did I imagine that?

"That's fantastic, well done April," Dawn says.

The song on my phone finishes and the next song comes on. Ed Sheeran and Elton John – 'Merry Christmas'. My heart sinks. Why can't I get rid of this song? I wonder if it means as much to Ben as it does to me.

I pick up my phone, wiping paint off my hands. Shit, it's nearly midday.

"I have to go," I say, half-relieved.

"Do you want me to finish this off? I can paint some cakes on the side and name it if you want?" Ben says.

"Sure," I say happy to get away.

◆ ◆ ◆

I practically run to the coffee shop. When I arrive, I'm so out of breath Emily gets me a glass of water and demands I sit down.

"What the fuck happened to you?" she demands.

"Ben... was there... and Paige," I say, huffing and puffing. I really need to get fitter.

"How cosy," Emily says sarcastically.

"They were painting the ice cream van together, but weirdly no one mentioned the engagement," I say.

"That's good isn't it? Maybe he didn't do it," Emily says. "Now is the time to tell him how you feel," she says.

"No, I can't do it. She is always around," I ask.

"I could do it for you?" she suggests.

I shake my head. "Not a chance. I think I should just get it into my head that that's it. We had our chance and we blew it. Second chances don't come in real life. It's just TV and films where they do. In real life we have to live with the consequences and I think this one is going to take a while to get over," I say miserably.

◆ ◆ ◆

I should cancel tonight. I'm not in the right head space at all. My thoughts are all about Ben and how much it hurts that he has moved on. That's not fair on James at all.

"So I think you should wear this dress with your boots," Tilly says, bringing out a strappy dress.

"No, I don't want to look like I tried too hard," I say.

"But you want to look like you made an effort," Emily says.

They look through my wardrobe and show me clothes. But none of them make me want to get dressed up.

"I think I should cancel," I say.

"Why? Because of Ben? Definitely not, what if James is the one and it takes you getting over Ben to realise that?" Emily says.

"I just don't feel right going out with James," I say.

"Then just wear jeans and one of your cute tops then," Tilly says, handing me one.

At least I don't look too dressed up and anyway, it's way too cold to wear dresses.

I pull on my skinny jeans, cute white button- up t-shirt and a grey cardigan. Okay, I look good.

"Let me straighten your hair," Emily says, sitting me down.

When I have finally been made over and my hair is straight, I hug both of them before I go out the door.

"Remember if you need to leave or you aren't having a good time, text us," Tilly says and they both kiss me on the cheek.

I arrive first. I find somewhere to sit and Harry

comes over. "What can I get you, love?" he asks.

"Just an orange juice," I say. I watch villagers out of the window driving home from work. Does James drive? I realise I don't know much about him at all. I move the hair out of my face and nervously look around. James isn't here yet and I am quite grateful for that.

"Hey," James says coming over. He is carrying a guitar bag on his back.

"You brought your guitar?" I ask. Will he play it? Do I want him to?

"Yes, I just came straight from band practice, so I apologise if I don't look the best," James says.

"That's okay," I say and gesture for him to sit down. He puts the bag on the seat and sits opposite me.

"So how was your day?" he asks me.

"It was fine," I say.

"Just fine," he asks. He tilts his head like he is trying to figure me out.

"Yes, I mean I worked and then I spent a little bit of it with you and well, that's it," I say.

"Yes, I love this strange little village. I haven't been back here since I was a child. But with my granddad not being well and my brother working away I had to come back. You probably don't remember us, they used to call me Jimbot at school because I was obsessed with robots and Tom was the quiet one," James says.

I laugh because I do remember. "No way it's you. It's cool that you are back," I say.

"Yeah, the doctor doesn't think my granddad has long left, so I wanted to be back here. You know, just spend what might be possibly our last Christmas as a family," James says.

"That's so sad," I say. He takes my hands across the table and I don't want to admit how disappointed I am that I don't feel anything.

"Yeah, but it's life isn't it? We have to live and enjoy it while we can," James says.

I nod. "Yes we do. I love your positivity," I say.

Harry comes over. "What can I get you, mate?" he asks James.

"Just water please," James says.

"Okay, just so you know couples karaoke starts soon, if you want to sign up. We are spinning a wheel for the songs to sing," Harry says.

"Ooh that sounds fun," I say.

"Totally, we should do that," James says.

"Sign us up, Harry," I say.

"Okay kiddos," Harry says and walks off.

'I've never sung on a date before... well, I've not dated much, other than when I was with Paige," James says.

"Yeah I heard that you used to be together?" I say.

"Yeah, she is really cool but she was super needy and I just can't have that when I am possibly going on tour with the band as soon as we sign with someone," James says.

I nod.

"That's so exciting and well, I am too busy to be needy," I say with a laugh. "I'm hoping to get this ice cream van fixed up and then I can do festivals."

"That van's cool. It's like the mystery machine but instead of a camper it serves cakes," James says.

A loud noise from the microphone interrupts us and we look over to Harry. He is standing in front of two microphones on stands with one in his hand.

"Hello everyone welcome to couples karaoke, if you still want to sign up the form is right here. We're going to go from the top to the bottom. First up we have Wendy and Ted," Harry says. Everyone claps as they spin the wheel.

"It's Endless Love, folks let's give them a round of applause," Harry says. We all clap as they sing. I look around. Dawn and Neil are here but there's no sign of Ben. Thank god. I don't need to see him right now.

"So what do you think we will sing?" James asks, finishing off his drink.

"Not a clue but I'm excited," I say.

"Me too," he says.

Wendy and Ted finish and we all clap for them.

"Okay, next up we have Neil and Dawn. Spin the wheel and see what song you'll sing," Harry says.

Neil spins the wheel and pulls his wife up to stand with him.

"Don't Go Breaking My Heart," Harry says. "Take it away."

"Do you want to dance?" James asks.

"Sure," I say and we stand up. He twirls me around and even with my arm on his shoulder and looking into his eyes, I don't feel much. Maybe that is just how it is in real life. It's not supposed to be like how it is in books. You just enjoy the other person's company and that is enough, and I am enjoying his company.

"Very nice, give Dawn and Neil a big round of applause. They do lots for our community," Harry says.

When they sit down, we stand on the dance floor. We're one of the only couples to be dancing but I don't care.

"I'm getting another drink," I say heading to the bar.

"Really? Haven't you had a glass of wine already?"

James asks. I just look at him. Is he really judging what I drink?

"Yes, I'm having another one," I say and put my order to Harry.

"Okay, April, but you are up next," Harry says.

I take my drink back to James.

"We're next," I say.

"Sounds good, I hope we aren't singing anything too soppy," he says.

"I'm not fussed, I just want to have a fun time," I say.

"Maybe you can sing and I can play my guitar. You want to hear me before the parade, don't you?" he asks.

"That would be lovely," I say and smile. You can't like everything about someone I guess. He must just have a strong opinion on drinking and I respect that.

"Okay, next up is April with her boyfriend, James," Harry says. "Come on up and spin the wheel."

I want to correct Harry. James isn't my boyfriend. We've been on one date.

"Spin it, spin it," I hear from one of the tables. I see Paige and Ben sitting with Ben's mum and dad. When did he arrive? I didn't see him.

I spin it and it lands on. 'Fairytale of New York.'

"Great," I say to James.

"Let me go and get my guitar," he says. The song starts and I am standing on my own. Everyone is watching and I am nervous. Oh god, what if James is terrible? He comes back and sits on a stool beside me. He lowers the microphone so he can play and sing.

He starts the song and the microphone squeaks. His voice is awful. It's the worst sound I have ever heard. I have never heard anyone sing like this before. I try to hide my shock as I sing my part. He strums along but it's like he is a child just playing with a guitar. He is plucking the strings any old way.

I am so grateful when the song is over.

"Give them a round of applause guys," Harry says.

I don't meet anyone's eyes. I am in fact so upset and embarrassed I want to go home.

Do I text Tilly and Emily? No, I will just try to enjoy the night.

"That was great, April but I am afraid I have to go home now. If I'm not in bed by ten I won't get enough sleep to get me through tomorrow," James says.

"Oh, okay," I say.

We walk out into the coldness silently. Did we just have the worse date? No of course not, this is all me. Well, the singing isn't. Maybe one day we will tell our kids how we did karaoke and it was awful. Yes, of course. *Give him a chance.* I say in my head as we reach my house.

We hover by my door. James smiles at me through the sleet, which is shining in the street lamp glow.

"I had a great time April," James says. He leans in closer to me and then kisses me on the head.

"Oh, me too," I say and I walk inside my house.

CHAPTER 16

It's the seventh of December. Mum is baking early this morning and instead of me helping I'm in the tiny cupboard in the back of the café, trying to sort out the Christmas music we are using at the parade.

After my strange date with James, I am avoiding Ben. I don't want to hear what he thought of James' singing. Why did I say yes to him being in the parade without hearing him? I also don't want to hear how Ben is truly loved up. It hurts so much to think that we could be happy together if we had managed to stay together. Another reason I regret leaving him.

I am just noting down song fifteen as 'Lonely This Christmas' when Ben opens the door.

"Ah, there you are. Anyone would think you're avoiding me," he says with a smile.

"No, I'm sorting the music out for the parade," I say, turning on song sixteen. 'One More Sleep'.

"How was your night out with James?" Ben asks.

"You were there, you saw him," I say defensively. I can't believe this is the first thing he says.

"Yeah, he can't sing a note or play the guitar and you have already booked him for the parade," Ben says.

"Yeah, if you were actually helping me we could have sorted this together," I say.

"I'm sorry, I have been busy with Paige. She wants to get married in February so it's a bit of a rush with wedding planning," Ben says. He is smiling my favourite smile where his eyes light up, and I feel fluttery and nervous. It's as if I'm a teenager again.

"I'm happy for you," I say.

"You will come to the wedding, won't you?" Ben asks.

"Urm," I say. What do I say? "Probably not I will be working."

"You can bring James if you want," he says.

"I don't think Paige will like that," I say.

"Why won't Paige like it?" he asks.

"Because they used to date. Didn't you know?" I ask. Shit, have I put my foot in it?

"I thought I heard them at the mistletoe event but I have been trying to forget that evening. I guess it doesn't really matter," he says.

Is he trying to forget that we kissed? Does that mean he did feel something?

We are silent as I continue writing down the songs. My eyes have clouded over and I feel the tears again. Why can't I stop crying?

"Ape, I know things between us haven't been the same and I'm sorry," Ben says. He fiddles with his hair again and I look down at the floor.

"It's okay," I say in a whisper.

"No, it isn't. I have been so busy I was even late to the meeting for Christ's sake," he says.

"Ben, it's really okay. We are nearly done with the parade and after that you can go back to your life," I say.

"But I want you in my life," he says.

"Ben, you are getting married and I can't shift these feelings that have resurfaced. I thought something happened the other day, it did for me at least and I don't want to do something to hurt you or Paige. I don't think we can be friends," I say.

He looks hurt. The same look he had when we were eighteen. The music fills the silence in the room and neither of us know what to say. At least I said it.

"Hello? Ben, what's taking you so long?" Emily opens the door and looks between us. I swear Ben is wiping his eyes.

"We are on our way," Ben says. The twisting in my gut tightens and I feel like I can't breathe.

I should say something to him at least. But I can't.

"Come on we have something to show you," Emily says taking my hand. I follow behind Ben into the car park where we've parked all of the floats.

There's glitter and tinsel everywhere. Mum has been busy decorating her float with Christmas drinks, and she'll be handing the real thing out to the crowds on the night. The back of the float has been painted as if it was the inside of the coffee shop and is decorated with lights.

I smile at everyone decorating their floats. They have really made an effort.

"I will take over, dude," I hear James say.

"Close your eyes," Emily says and I do. I feel around and a cold hand takes mine.

"We've got you," James says and they lead me to the float.

"Ben, Paige, everyone, go and stand over there," Emily orders.

"Okay, open your eyes," Tilly says. I do and the first thing I do is gasp. The ice cream van is painted in the purple colour I started with, and someone has painted a pink cupcake that is displayed on the top of it.

There are tears in my eyes - and I'm not sure

whether they are from what I said to Ben or because all my friends have done this for me.

"Did you all do this?" I ask, looking at each of them.

"Ben has been in charge of all of this. He has been painting the floats and ordering us around," Emily says.

I look at Ben. Why did I tell him I don't want to be friends anymore? Why did I tell him how I feel? What is wrong with me?

"It was no big deal, that's what you do for friends," Ben says with a shrug. He won't look at me.

"I can't believe you did all of this," I say to Ben.

Everyone in the parade throws their arms around me including Paige.

"Don't ever say I don't do anything for you," Ben says. The air between us is awkward. Ben runs his hand through his hair. "I've got to head back to work."

"You aren't staying?" Paige asks.

"Nah, I have a car coming in with brake problems in about twenty minutes," Ben says.

We watch him leave, not looking back at us.

"I will talk to him," Paige says, looking as confused as everyone else.

"It's okay, you don't have to," I say.

I look at Emily who is mouthing *'what happened?'* and I shrug.

"Ben really is a good person, April, he wanted to do all of this so he wouldn't let you down," Paige says and I nod. I feel the tears in my eyes. I am an awful person.

"I know," I say quietly. I watch Ben leave and then I open the back door of the ice cream and it's sparkling clean. One of the freezers has been taken out and an oven has been fitted and shelves have been drilled into the walls of the van. I smile through the tears.

"Can I come in?" James asks.

"Sure," I say. He leans against the door. I open the little shutters and see my friends outside.

Emily is first at the shutters.

"Are you going to tell me what the fuck was that?" she says.

"I told Ben how I felt and that I can't be his friends," I whisper. Luckily James isn't paying attention. Not that I owe him anything, anyway. We've been on one date.

"Ouch, terrible timing. He was really excited this morning to show you what he has been doing," Emily says.

"I know and now I feel awful," I say.

"You should do," Emily says.

Tilly joins Emily at the shutters.

"I can't believe he did all of this and you all kept it quiet," I say. I feel so bad. Why did I have to say something? I should have taken my advice and just kept quiet. At least when we were friends I could see him and talk to him.

"We've been doing it on a rota that Ben organised all week when we've had time. Emily has been coming to help on her break, James has been permanently here doing each coat of paint with Ben, and his dad helped fit in the oven and shelves for you," Emily says.

"I really appreciate it," I say. James holds his hand out for me. I take it but I definitely don't feel a spark between us. Instead I feel intense guilt and butterflies.

"Yeah well Ben is a great organiser," James says. "And I want to say that I really enjoyed our drink together last night."

"Yes, you didn't tell us how your date went," Emily says, looking between us.

"It was great," James says, smiling at me. "Though April drank like a pirate."

"Yeah," I say.

Being here with James feels so wrong. It should be Ben here. I should be thanking him and looking around the floats with him but like always I pushed him away again.

I sigh looking at James while he explores the cake van. Do I want to go out with James again? I think I should give him another chance. Maybe he was nervous before. I need to fall out of love with Ben and what better than to find someone else?

"So you are going to bake in here?" James asks. Interrupting my thoughts.

"I was going to yeah, do you like baking?" I ask him.

"I haven't really done it before," he says.

"April are you in there?" Mum asks me.

"I am here. James is here too," I say.

"Hi Mrs, urm April's Mum," James says and holds his hand out to her.

"Hi, James I am Mrs Edwards but call me Liz. I was just saying April if you want to take your break now, that's fine," Mum says.

"Yes please. I am going to get some baking ingredients. Would you like to bake with me?" I ask James.

"Sure why not?" James says. His face lights up and I smile. He is a nice man and I need to chill out a bit. Maybe spending less time with Ben is a good thing.

I follow Mum back into the coffee shop and gather up bowls and ingredients.

"Please say thank you to Ben for helping to

organise all of this," Mum says as I'm on my way out of the coffee shop.

"I'm back. I was thinking because it's nearly Christmas, would you like to make mince pies?"

"You will have to show me but remember I can't eat them. I am vegan," he says.

"Oh, you should have said. I would have bought vegan mince," I say. I can make myself like James can't I? It isn't like we are going to get married right now, is it?

I hand him a bowl. Our hands brush again when I give him his ingredients and there's no spark again. Am I disappointed? I think I am. But I am nearly thirty and I can't be alone forever.

CHAPTER 17

"Just follow me," I say, measuring out my ingredients. I give James the flour and measure the butter out. He copies me.

"So now we need to make it into breadcrumbs," I say, showing him how and he copies me. We work in almost silence apart from the noise outside the van and I can't help thinking about Ben and what I said to him.

I get a towel for us and we wipe our hands.

"Thank you," he says. "But I can't eat this."

"That's fine," I say.

"I'm sorry," he says. "I am having a good time though."

Now I feel bad. I look out of the flap window and see Paige outside talking to Emily.

"Me too," I say.

I wash up and make sure the surfaces are clean.

"I forgot how much I like this little village," James says.

"Yeah, I feel the same way," I say. He takes my hand and smiles at me. I smile back. Even though I'm not in love with James, I can still get to know him and enjoy his company.

"I don't think Paige's boyfriend likes me," he says.

"Maybe not, but why do you care?" I ask.

"I don't really. I am just wondering what Paige sees in him," James says. "She has always been ambitious and hardworking but she even told me since she's been dating him she has cut down her hours."

"Maybe that's just what love is," I say. I don't like the thought of Ben in love -well I do, but not with Paige. Annoyingly enough I have nothing bad to say about her at all.

"Don't get me wrong, I love, *love* but I don't think that is love. What we used to have was," James says.

I can't help frowning at him. Does he still love Paige?

"What about us?" I say to him. Do I even want an us?

"Well, we have only been dating for a week I think it's a bit soon to say," James says.

"Yeah," I say. He pulls me with his arm to him and I can't help swallowing. Do I want to kiss him?

"Hello, April, are you still here?" Paige asks.

"I am," I say. I pull away from James and open the door, thankful for the cool air. It's a little stuffy in here.

"I have to go back to work now," she says. "I wanted to ask if you want to come to the pub with me and Ben tonight."

"Maybe," I say.

"You are welcome to join us. Bring James, it could be like a double date," she says.

I see her looking at James and I recognise that look. It's the same look I give when I am around Ben.

◆ ◆ ◆

The mince pies are on the rack cooling down with the shutters and windows wide open.

"Are you selling your mince pies here today?" Mrs Barrow asks. I remember the elderly Mrs Barrow always giving the children candy canes for Christmas.

"No, just testing the waters for now. Have one-but it might be a bit hot," I say, giving her one.

She takes it. "Thank you."

I look back James. He is too busy chatting to someone and I can't help think Ben would be thrilled for me.

I text Ben that I gave away my first mince pie from

the van.

Great, is all Ben replies. I think I really hurt him.

◆ ◆ ◆

I'm so nervous. I should have said no. I'm just hurting myself by going out with Ben. But I do owe him an apology.

"Hi," I say when he walks in and spots me. I am very grateful for him being on his own.

"Hi, I'm not sure why Paige wanted to do this," Ben says.

"Where is Paige?" I ask.

"She's just finished work. She's on her way now," he says. "Where's James?"

"No idea," I say with a shrug.

Harry comes over and we order our drinks. James texts me just in time I arrived what drinks he and Paige want. And I order them.

"Sorry we are late," Paige says and sits down next to Ben. James comes and sits next to me and kisses me on the cheek

"That's okay babe," Ben says.

"I thought it would be nice you know, for all of us to go out," Paige says.

"Yeah, totally," James says.

Harry comes back. "Here are your drinks. Two sparkling waters."

"You remembered?" Paige asks.

"Of course I did," James says.

"Beer and wine," Harry interrupts them looking between us.

Ben passes me my glass and takes his own beer.

"So I just want to tell everyone that I'm leaving the garage after Christmas," Ben says.

My mouth is hanging wide open. I don't know what to say to that. Paige looks at him. She doesn't look happy.

"Do you think I'm crazy for doing it?" Ben asks. I'm not sure who he is asking.

"No," I say.

"Yes," Paige says. We say it at the same time.

"Is it what you want, man?" James asks.

"Yes, I have actually been thinking about it for a while, but organising the parade and painting the floats has given me a new purpose and I feel like I need to follow that," Ben says.

"But Ben you won't be able to live on the money just from painting," Paige says.

"But babe, I have been saying how much I hate my job for ages now," Ben says.

"I thought you were just going through a rough patch," Paige says.

"Why can't you do both?" James asks.

"I've been in denial about what I've wanted to do. I'm sorry Paige, but I think I have decided," Ben says.

Paige sits back with her arms crossed.

"I don't like this," Paige says.

"Well, this is a familiar conversation," James says.

Paige shoots him a look and I look at Ben, puzzled.

"What's going on?" Ben asks them.

"The reason Paige and I split is because she didn't believe that I could get a recording contract and make enough money," James says.

"It isn't that I don't want you to follow your dreams, I just think you should be realistic," Paige says. Her face is red.

"My advice is just do what you need to man, life is too short," James says.

"Thank you, James," Ben says.

"I agree," I say to James and he smiles. Ugh. I really need to tell James I don't want to go out with him again. Maybe after the parade is over I can tell him.

"Actually, I will have a glass of wine," Paige says getting up.

"Really?" James asks.

"Yeah, come with me," Paige says.

"Ben, I am so sorry about what I said," I say leaning close to him. My heart is beating so fast.

"Which part: the part where you don't want to be friends, or the part where you said you have feelings, or even the part where I helped organise the parade which is what you wanted me to do and then you drop the other two bombshells on me?" Ben asks.

Shit.

"All the above," I say.

"I'm sorry too, I am sorry I pushed you away when you first came back and I am sorry I made a mess of our friendship and then I'm sorry I kissed you, well, I'm not sorry, but now you are dating this man, and well - he is seriously weird. And I am sorry I left earlier before you saw inside the van," Ben says.

"I wish you had been there," I say.

"Me too," he says. "I just didn't know how to handle not being friends. It absolutely kills me that I can't be friends with you."

"I do want to be friends," I say. I want to shout that I love him and always have but I can't.

"So let's be friends," he says with a big smile.

◆ ◆ ◆

"So what painting do you do, Ben?" James asks.

They are sat back on the table and weirdly we've moved around so James and Paige are sat together and I am sat next to Ben.

"Mostly buildings, murals. Anything really. I've got savings and well, I am hoping when Paige and I are married she will come and live with my mum and dad until we buy our own place," Ben says.

"We won't if you don't have a job," Paige says. "Please, please consider it. I want us to have space."

"I know it isn't ideal but at least we will be together," Ben says.

She sighs.

"Can we please change the subject? I would like to toast to my perfect van," I say.

"I was inside there earlier and it's pretty rocking," James says.

"It looks amazing," Paige says.

"You were in there?" Ben asks, looking between us.

I hold my glass up and they tap theirs to it. "Yes he was," I say.

"We baked, I would say it's a bit too small but it's pretty cool," James says.

"Well you both looked cosy in there," Paige says.

I'm too worried to look up at Ben. I know he is looking at me.

"Anyway, April I want to talk about the rest of the parade. The floats will be done in the next couple of days," Ben says.

"We have the music mostly sorted and the stage is ready. We do still have to decorate the park though," I say I force myself to look up at him and when our eyes meet. I feel that same feeling, the one I was hoping would be there when I baked with James.

"Yes we do," Ben says.

I look around at the crowded pub. Everyone seems to be celebrating something and the place is buzzing. Harry has brought the karaoke out again and people are queuing for their own turn.

"Does anyone fancy a go?" Ben asks around the table.

"Hmm, I'm not sure. I know how much you hate karaoke," I say.

"He has never hated it with me," Paige says.

"I will do it," James says.

"I'll do it if you do, Ape," Ben says and I feel the butterflies. He would do it for me.

"Okay then. It will be ace," I say and smile.

"I'm going to put us all down then. We can couple

up, do one and then switch it up," Paige says.

"Sounds great," I say. Is Paige trying to find reasons to spend time with James or am I paranoid?

Paige leaves the table and James goes with her.

"Hi you two," Emily comes over with her own drink. A cocktail by the looks of it.

"Hi, Em I didn't know you would be here," I say, looking around for Tilly.

"She's meeting me here. Do you think I look nice? It's sort of a date," she says, whispering the last part.

"You look gorgeous," I say.

She's wearing a white vest with a sequinned beige cardigan and jeans. She looks stunning and the light from the pub bounces off her sequins, making her glow.

"This looks cosy with you two and them two," she says.

"We are on a double date," I say.

"Hmm," she says and frowns.

We see Paige and James coming back and she dashes off.

"So, I've written our names down and brought the music list over. What would everyone like to sing?" Paige asks.

Ben shuffles closer to me and I smell his

aftershave. I have butterflies again.

"Oh my god, do you remember this from school?" I ask, stopping on a page. Ben lets out a laugh.

"Oh yes," he says. "We can do that if you want, but I need a few more drinks first."

CHAPTER 18

The karaoke queue is going down fast and Harry comes over to tell us we are next. Tilly and Emily join us at our table.

"We were going to sing but we decided against it," Emily says.

"Well, I would have but you weren't interested," Tilly says. They are holding hands under the table and are acting like we haven't noticed. We have and I think it's cute.

"Why don't you sing with us?" Ben asks.

"It's James and me first," Paige says and I notice the look Emily is giving me.

"I would rather eat my own sick, cheers," Emily says.

"What's everyone singing?" Tilly asks.

"We are singing a classic," I say. Ben nods and I get the look again from my sister.

"Our favourite song," Paige says to James.

I can't help looking at Ben who seems oblivious to

the red flags. Is Paige still in love with James?

"I'm just going to the loo, I'll be back before it's our turn," Ben says getting up and going to the toilet.

"Up next we have Paige and James singing 'NSYNC – I Want You Back'," Harry announces.

They stand up and sing. James still can't sing a note.

"How are they being this obvious?" Emily asks me.

"No idea. Ben seems oblivious. I saw them Emily, when James was baking with me. The way they were looking at each other like well, they loved each other," I say.

The way James and Paige are singing together with their arms around each other. They are also holding hands. Where the fuck is Ben?

Ben comes back as they are finished. He missed the entire thing.

"What did I miss?" he asks.

"Paige and James were singing," I say.

"Was it bad again?" he asks.

"Yes, I think you should ask them about it," I say.

"Why?" he asks.

"Okay everyone, our final singers of the night are Ben and April singing 'Sisqo – Thong Song'," Harry announces and we stand up. Tilly and Emily both scream and cheer for us.

I down my drink, feeling more confident. Tilly and Emily get up as well.

The song begins and Ben starts. I join in and we dance together, shaking our bodies like we used to when we danced together. Ben takes my hand and twirls me around and I sing my part. Tilly and Emily join us in singing with microphones to the last chorus. I know I'm drunk and all I'm thinking about is kissing Ben. I can't kiss Ben.

The song finishes as Ben twirls me against him. The world has stopped around us and I look up at him. We are both sweaty from dancing and our noses are so close they are touching. I swallow as I pull away from him. I'm shaking. I seriously need another drink.

"I'm, urm, going to get another drink," I say.

"Well shit. He definitely knows you meant what you said the other day now," Tilly says. We are all standing at the bar waiting for drinks.

"I daren't go back to the table," I say, looking at them. The three of them are deep in conversation. Paige turns her head and glares at me. Shit.

"You have to admit you looked good up there and it isn't like she is innocent," Emily says.

"You need to tell him what they were doing and what you think is going on," Tilly says.

"I can't. He won't believe me if I do and anyway, I only have suspicions I haven't seen anything happen," I say. "Answer me this: if she wasn't here, do you think he would have kissed me?"

"Yes," they both say.

"But it's wrong right? He has a girlfriend?"

"Don't you have a boyfriend?" Emily says.

"James, no not a chance," I say.

"Then yes it's wrong, but you told him how you feel and he still danced with you," Emily says.

"Exactly," Tilly agrees.

"I'm so confused. Why would he dance with me and almost kiss me when he has a fiancé?

"Because he's a man and he doesn't know what he wants," Tilly says.

"Ha, I have a pretty good idea what he wants," Emily chimes in.

"He's been spending time with me behaving like he's single and organising the parade to show to me and then he fucking proposed to her after he almost kissed me," I say.

I feel frustrated and angry. No wonder I don't know what is happening. Why does Ben want us to be friends so badly? I told him how I felt and he nearly kissed me again tonight. Is that what friends do? And why did he do all the floats on his own is he trying to impress me?

"Come on, let's walk you home," Tilly says

interrupting my thoughts and helping me to stand up.

"I'm just going back to the coffee shop. I need to bake for the school nativity and the parade," I say.

"Will you be okay on your own?" Emily asks.

"Yes," I say.

I walk over to the table where Ben, James and Paige are and let James know this time I definitely don't want to go out with him. I walk towards the door and glance back once more. Ben locks eyes with me and I let the tears out as I head out.

◆ ◆ ◆

It's Monday morning, the day of the school nativity and the last week of term. It's six am and I've just flicked the sign from shut to open with my ice cream van parked out front, cooking my apple pies and chocolate cupcakes.

I sit down for a few minutes while the timer ticks and think about everything. I'm so excited for the parade on Saturday. Ben hasn't spoken to me since the karaoke and I haven't really seen Paige. I don't really know what that means for mine and Ben's friendship but we still have this parade to finish. I need help with setting up in the park.

Tilly and Emily walk in. Emily is sharing shifts with me so I can continue baking for the parade and Tilly has to go to school.

"Morning." Tilly stands at the counter, waiting to be served. I give them privacy as Emily makes her a drink and they kiss.

I head out to the ice cream van. The street lights are blurred by the rain. I open the back of my van and bring the cakes out of the oven. My chocolate cupcakes look and smell amazing, and I can't wait to serve them up today at the nativity and on Saturday for the parade.

I bring them into the coffee shop and Tilly and Emily eye them up.

"Are they for the children after the nativity?" Tilly asks.

"Yes and I don't want to find any missing," I say.

"As if I would," Tilly says, acting shocked.

"So is there any news on…you know?" Emily asks me.

I shake my head. "Nothing, and I still have to decorate the park for the parade. I've got the balloons that all need blowing up and the bunting. Everything needs to be in the park for Wednesday in time for our stage rehearsal," I say.

"Is James still performing?" Emily asks.

"Yes, he is really excited about it," I say. I am dreading it. Although At least he didn't seem fussed after we kind of broke up.

"At least it's Christmas songs so everyone will be

too drunk to care," Emily says.

"I just have so much to do and I'm not sure how I will get on with it without Ben," I say.

"We can help you, of course, and everyone in the village. If you want me to spread the word around to help decorate the village, we can?" Tilly offers.

"Yes, please. Do you think I should go and ask Ben if he's still helping me?" I ask, looking over the road at the garage. I haven't seen it open since Thursday. Has he quit his job already?

"Hmm, I'm not sure. If he's ignoring you that's his problem, but then again he said he would help you with all of the parade, not just the floats," Emily says.

"Or go and tell his mum and dad," Tilly says.

I laugh. I could and they would be annoyed with him.

"I would go and see him first. Ooh, speaking of the devil," Emily says, nudging towards the door.

Ben is standing outside in his raincoat with his hood up crossing the empty road towards the garage. He doesn't once turn around.

"He is avoiding you," Tilly says standing by the window.

"Please don't shout at him," I say quickly when Tilly opens her mouth.

"Don't you want to know what his problem is?" she asks.

"We danced together and nearly kissed, that was our problem," I say.

"I wish you had kissed, and then he could tell you he feels the same about you and you can be together," Emily says, bringing over her drink.

"He is getting married. Of course he doesn't feel the same way about me," I say.

"He does, he just knows he can't do anything because he's getting married so ignoring you is the easier option," Emily says.

"I still need his help though just for the rest of the week," I say.

"I haven't seen you like this in years," Tilly says.

"Mh-hm." A voice behind me makes me jump. It's Ben. Oh shit, did he hear us?

"Sorry," I squeak, turning to face him. His face is wet from the rain.

"Can I have a black coffee, no syrup, and a few minutes of your time?" he asks.

I bite my lip, spinning to face Emily who is already shooing me to go. I make the drink, dropping everything as I go. I don't know why I'm so flustered.

"You need to chill out. He wants to talk, that's a

good thing," Tilly says next to me. We are behind the door and Ben can't hear us.

"Is it though? What if he wants to tell me he can't be friends because of Paige?" I say. I ache at the thought of that.

"Or maybe he's come to apologise," Tilly says.

I walk back to Ben and give him his drink.

"Come on," he says, walking towards the door. I follow him, with my hands in my pockets.

CHAPTER 19

I am more nervous than when I first came back. Heck, even more nervous than when I had my meeting with Milly's and got a full time job there.

Ben crosses the road. The sun is coming up now and I can already see parents doing the school run.

Ben unlocks the garage and we walk inside. I hover around the door awkwardly, the memories of Friday on my mind.

"Ben I'm sorry for what happened but I still need you to help me with the parade," I say.

"I know, and we will talk about that. But I'm stuck in a rut."

I look up, instantly curious about what he is going to say.

"Is this about James and Paige?" I ask, wondering if he has finally clocked on.

"Ape, after what happened Friday, I am so confused about how I feel about you. I'm the one who is sorry," he says, perching on his desk. I want to take his hands and tell him I love him but that won't help anything so I stay by the door.

"Ben, I'm also sorry. I should never have dragged you up to do karaoke," I say.

He shakes his head. "Ape, Paige doesn't want me to see you again. After the parade we are going to move into her parents' house. I need to make this work with her," Ben says. He runs his hands through his hair and turns his back to me. I want to slide my arms around him.

It's exactly what I thought would happen and it feels like I've been punched in the gut.

"I don't know what to say," I whisper, barely audible.

"I spent so many years wishing you were coming back and then when you did I wasted the time we could have been friends again with anger. God I was so mad at you. I thought when Paige came along last Christmas I had finally got over you and we clicked. She is amazing. The way she lights up when she smiles. And her laugh is infectious. But there's just one problem I have now, she isn't you," he says.

I really don't know what to say. I let him go and he found someone and one day maybe I will find someone.

"I'm sorry for the way we left things," I say.

"I know, like I said I was angry with you for

coming back. How dare you interrupt what I thought was my perfect life," he says.

"It sounds pretty good to me," I say.

"It has been. Well, until about two weeks ago but I'm sorry for kissing you and I am sorry for wanting to kiss you more than anything. I've found someone Ape, I actually have all my shit together," he says and I laugh. "So why aren't I happy?"

"I don't know Ben, but if you need me to stay away to be happy with Paige then I will," I say. "Just please help me with the rest of the parade."

Ben swallows and I look up at him to see tears in his eyes. "I'm sorry Ape," he says, his voice breaking.

I swallow the lump in my throat. "Don't be, we had something amazing, but it isn't our time now," I say.

I turn around, heading out the door letting the tears come fast. I can't go back to work again, not for a while, so I put my hands in my pocket and walk out of the door towards the park. If I start setting the park up with balloons, then it might take my mind off of Ben. I reach the park and sit on the soggy bench.

I look out to the distance and see a hut has been built. The parade isn't until Saturday. I suppose bringing the animals early might get them settled in.

I get up curiously, hearing noises that I assume are the reindeer. Until I walk to the door and see Paige lying on a blanket naked with James on top of her. Shit. Now the question is - do I tell Ben?

◆ ◆ ◆

"Of course you need to tell him," Emily whispers as we sit in the school hall. It smells like school dinners. The children have all come onto the stage and we clap each of them. There's no sign of Ben anywhere.

"Emily, after this morning, I don't think I can be the one to say anything. Hey, I'm in love with you and your girlfriend is shagging James," I say in a mocking voice.

"Well he can't marry her can he? I knew we had every right to be suspicious on Friday," she says.

"I know but how will it look coming from me?" I say, whining.

"It will look like you're jealous," Emily says after a minute.

"Exactly. Ben has already said Paige doesn't want me hanging around him," I say.

"Because that is a healthy relationship," Emily says and nudges towards the chairs. I look up and Ben is there with Paige.

"Babe, can we sit somewhere else?" Paige asks, giving me a fake smile. I roll my eyes and look at Emily.

"Oh, okay," Ben says and we lock eyes. My insides are swirling and I'm so fed up of crying over Ben today that I don't think I have any more tears in me.

"Bye Ben." Emily waves to him.

"He's completely under her thumb. And she must be paranoid about him because it's her screwing around," I say.

"Wow, you can't tell an adult not to talk to someone. Especially when you are doing the parade together," Emily says.

"Yeah, he has basically told me he can't do any more of it," I say.

"Since when?" Emily asks.

"Since our conversation earlier and he told me he feels the same and then I see his fiancé shagging James," I say.

"Someone else needs to tell him. Someone who doesn't have feelings for him," Emily says.

"Like you?" I ask hopeful.

"No, I'm too closely linked to you, it would still come across badly, But I mean someone like his mum, or our mum, or someone in the village," she says.

"Everyone in the village likes her," I say.

I'm not sure how she has managed it but even our own mum said she's a nice girl and they make a good couple," Emily says.

"I know, and they are getting married in two months," I say.

We wave at Tilly, who comes on the stage to introduce all of the children so they can take a bow. We clap along and Emily does that mouth whistle thing I can't do.

"Thank you to everyone who helped paint our sets and who joined in helping with our costumes, and to all of you parents at home. Please enjoy our little village refreshments before you leave," Tilly says and I realise this is my cue to leave.

Emily stays behind with Tilly and I head out to my ice cream van to give out cakes.

As soon as I open the flap door, there's a queue for my cakes and gingerbread that I baked specifically for today.

"I am hoping to organise my son's birthday party in a couple of weeks. Can I give you my details and we can discuss it?" one of the mums asks. She introduces herself as Chantelle and her sons name is Harrison.

"I was thinking about doing parties," I say, taking her card.

"It's just the cutest thing ever," she gushes.

"Hey, what did you think of the nativity?" Tilly comes over and hugs me. "This stall is the talk of the school. Everyone is asking whether it be booked for parties."

"We loved it of course. I know. I'm doing so well I think I might need to buy myself a diary," I say and she laughs.

"I'm thrilled for you," she says.

"Thanks," I say. "But did you see them snogging?" I sigh. Why did I have to see that? And why did no one stop them in a school?

"Yes, the head teacher has had a word. You know, because of the children and all. So what happened when you went over there earlier?" she asks. I give her some gingerbread and put the money in a little drawer I have. I really need to get a proper till put in.

"So, Ben wanted us to talk, and he told me he loves me but he wants to make it work with Paige, so we can't be friends and he can't do the parade either," I say taking a breath.

"Wow so where did you go after? Because you didn't come back for ages." Tilly asks.

"I went to the park to blow up some balloons. The reindeer hut was there and well...James and Paige were having sex," I say.

Tilly looks at me wide-eyed. "Did you tell Ben?" she asks.

"How can I? He isn't going to believe me, is he," I say. My shoulders slump.

A voice clears and I spin around to face Ben.

"I never had you down as vindictive," he says. "How can you say she is cheating on me? Paige would never do that."

"Ben, please," I say. I want to go after him, but a queue forms. I sigh, watching him walk out.

"What do I do now?" I ask Tilly. My stomach is all knotted and I feel sick. Surely he would know I wouldn't lie about that.

CHAPTER 20

Of course it's raining. I curse the sky. I can't stay in bed all morning even though I haven't really slept for two days.

Since Ben heard me on Monday, he has been purposely avoiding me, sending his mum and dad to help me with the parade, so at least I have had help. Everyone was more than happy to chip in of course, but I thought this was our project.

It's six and I'm not opening the coffee shop for once. I head down to the coffee shop with my umbrella sheltering me the entire time and open the door. The warmth hits me straight away.

"Hi April darling," Mum says cautiously.

"Hi Mum," I say.

"I just want to say something. Now, please don't be angry, but it's been a couple of days. Why not go over there and say you are sorry," she says.

"Mum, I haven't done anything wrong. I'm telling the truth but no one believes me," I say. I take my coat off.

"I'm sorry I just don't think Paige would do that," she says.

"Then you have her all wrong. She's pulled the wool over all of your eyes," I say.

"April, this is a big accusation. You are hurt and that is understandable after what happened," she says.

"It isn't an accusation, and it hurts that you don't believe me," I say.

It's been like this since Monday. No one believes my word against Paige's. She is obviously blinding everyone. Well, except for Tilly and Emily who know I would never lie about this. Ben made up his mind about who he wants, so why would I lie to get him when he chose someone else?

"April, it isn't that I don't want to believe you. She is engaged to Ben. Why would she throw that away? Mum says.

I shrug, wanting to end the conversation. I hate that everyone is acting like I've done something bad.

"Right, I'm going to get my float ready for the practice parade," she says and leaves.

Emily comes in with boxes of ingredients.

I wipe my eyes. "I'm sorry, Ape," she whispers.

"It's okay, but I think it was a mistake coming back," I say.

"Don't say that," she says. "I need my big sister."

"Em, you've done amazing since I've been gone. All I've done is upset everyone and got in the way. I have my van, I can make a living from it hopefully," I say.

Emily puts the box down and hugs me. "I'm sorry this village has made you feel like this."

"It's okay, but I've been gone too long to really belong back here. I've organised a lot of this parade on my own, so I think I will just slip out after Saturday," I say, feeling the tears fall onto her shoulder.

"I really don't want you to go," she says, sobbing on me. I feel her body shaking and I instantly feel bad.

"I know but I don't want to see them every day-and the villagers that don't believe me," I say.

Emily pulls away and wipes her face. "We should get moving to the town centre," she says.

I nod, getting in my ice cream van with her.

◆ ◆ ◆

When we arrive, all of the floats are already at the starting point in a row with each of the drivers aboard.

James is setting up the stage at the park so he can do a microphone test and tune the instruments.

I set up the ice cream van between Mum's coffee shop and Emily's crafting float. She's spent a lot of time making little Christmas decorations that anyone can buy after the parade.

Neil and Dawn are going around everyone, making sure they are okay. Two floats down, I see Ben with Paige. Tilly is in the float behind us prepping the children, who are thrilled they have the afternoon off of school to attend the practice.

Today is dress rehearsal too for the children, so it's the first time they are in their angel and star costumes. Everyone seems to be in a good mood.

I do a last check with the villagers in their floats to make sure everyone is okay and everything is working. I reach Ben and he doesn't give me eye contact but nods. I'm grateful when I reach Tilly and she gives me a hug. "You're amazing, ignore the haters."

I wipe away the tear coming down my cheek and signal for the floats to start. I follow them and guide them down the roads that have already been closed off for this afternoon and the music blasts through the streets. Crowds have formed already they see us and we wave. Some of the crowds join in with us and dance with the floats.

When we reach halfway, we do float checks to make sure everyone has petrol and everyone is okay and then carry on until we get to the park.

❖ ❖ ❖

At the park, all of the floats park up. I open my ice cream van to sell the gingerbread I made for everyone in the car park and Mum serves them all coffee. I sit on the bench with Tilly and Emily.

"Can you be with me tonight please?" she says holding my hand.

"Of course, but why?" I ask Emily, looking between them.

"I want to come out to Mum and Dad after work," she says.

I nod. "Of course." I hug her. "So are you two a thing now?"

"We are taking it slow," Tilly says and we all hold hands. I love my sister and best friend.

"I'm so pleased for you both," I say.

Ben and Paige come over. "Urm, so thank you for the gingerbread," Ben says, playing with his hair.

"It's okay," I say.

"OMG you gave her the look," Paige says, putting her hands on her hips. "Why would you look at her like that?" she says and gives me a dirty look before disappearing.

"Sorry Paige, I didn't realise I had," Ben says and I look at the girls, shaking my head.

"Why does everyone think the sun shines out of her arse?" I ask.

"Oh, yeah about that," Tilly says, her eyes lighting up.

"We are going to get evidence that she is shagging James. It's not fair that everyone is treating you so badly," Emily says.

"I know but she is cunning. She won't let you see her," I say.

"You did," Emily says.

"It's true, she has timed it all amazingly so it looks like you are jealous," Tilly says.

"I'm not jealous. I mean I still like Ben, but I'm okay. I am going to make a new start for myself," I say.

"I don't want you to leave town," Emily says.

"Please don't leave town," Tilly says.

I take in a sharp breath. "Guys, I love you and I will come and visit all of the time, but I won't be called a liar and given dirty looks over something I didn't do," I say. "I don't want to be known as the girl who is forever pining for her ex."

"It's absolute crap that no one believes you," Emily says.

"It is, and I don't want to leave," I say.

Mum comes over with another drink. "Well done

April, practice went amazingly. I can't wait till Saturday."

"Thanks Mum, it's gone pretty well," I say.

"Yes it has. Mr and Mrs Thomas wanted to have a word with you. They are so impressed with your organisation skills that they want to bring you into the committee," Mum says beaming. She looks proud of me.

"That's a reason to stick around isn't it?" Emily asks.

"What does she mean, April?" Mum asks. She's gone from beaming to frowning with lines on her forehead.

"Mum, I didn't want to say anything yet but I'm not sure I can stay in this village," I say.

"Is this because of Ben?" she asks.

"Yes and the fact no one believes me and I keep getting given dirty looks from people who used to really like me in this town. Ben has completely given up on the parade and if it wasn't for all of you, we would never have set up the park. And no one is mad at him," I say.

"You know he isn't worth it if he makes you feel like this, you shouldn't be the one leaving town," she says.

"Yeah, but it hurts that even you don't believe me," I say.

Mum looks at us all. "I'm sorry April. It is really unfortunate timing."

"That's why no one believed me," I say.

"I don't want you to feel like you have to leave because no one believed you. I didn't realise it meant so much to you," Mum says.

"So will you please stay now?" Emily begs.

"Maybe, but let's see how everyone else is," I say.

"Ben's mum and dad are offering you an amazing opportunity. They wouldn't be doing that if they didn't like you," Mum says.

"And everyone who helped with the parade did it because they like you," Tilly says.

"I think it's more that they wanted to keep the tradition going than anything," I say.

"Maybe, but you had everyone behind you. Dirty looks or not, they all gave you their free time to help," Mum says.

"Right, I have to go back to work. Will you be okay?" Tilly asks.

"Yes, I'll be fine," I say.

I feel myself softening. That is what this little village is about. Everyone has always helped everyone since I was little.

"I'm leaving Emily to close Brew and Chill tonight. And Mr Thomas wants to talk to you," Mum says.

CHAPTER 21

I head across the field and glance into the pen. Surely they aren't still in there. They wouldn't be this obvious.

"What are you doing?" Ben says behind me, making me jump.

"I was just wondering whether the reindeer will be here before I go home," I say.

I shouldn't have to explain myself. "What are you doing here?" I ask accusingly. I wrongly look up at him, feeling wiggly in my stomach. Why does he still make me feel like this even after all of this shit?

"I just came by to congratulate you. The rehearsal went amazing and I'm sorry I didn't help with the set up. Of course I want to be friends but Paige means a lot to me," Ben says.

"Thank you and don't worry about not being involved. It won't matter soon anyway because I've decided I might not stick around," I say.

He looks up at me and I swallow. His eyes look full

of tears. "You're leaving again?" he asks.

"Might be, but I will be okay. I just can't deal with the village accusing me of trying to break you and Paige up," I say.

"Is that why you're leaving, because a few people have said that?" he asks.

"Try everyone. Even people who regularly come into Brew and Chill are avoiding me now. I can't be around people that think I would do that. And you didn't exactly defend me," I say.

"I know. I have really messed everything up," he says.

"Why can't you see how toxic it all is?" I say.

"Paige isn't toxic. She cares a lot about me," Ben says.

"She cares so much that she has stopped you having friends in case you cheat, when it's her who's shagging her ex," I say. "I would have thought you'd want to know, considering you are getting married,"

I see Paige walking across the road towards the coffee shop.

"I don't believe you," he says and I wave to Emily who is walking my way.

"Fine, but don't cry to me when it all goes wrong," I say.

Emily reaches me. "Come and walk with me, I've got to lock up and I'll meet you at the house," Emily says and we start walking out of the park.

"Still want me to be there tonight?" I ask.

"Yes," she says. I take her hand and squeeze it.

"I'm here for you," I say.

◆ ◆ ◆

It's Saturday. The day of the parade, and although the sky is grey the rain is holding off for now. I opened early with Emily, who is still nervous after she told our parents about her and Tilly. Dad of course hugged her but Mum hasn't really mentioned it since. I'm not really sure if it's because she's been busy or she isn't happy, but Dad's told Emily to give her time.

"Are you excited for today?" Emily asks.

"Yes, I just wish things were different between Ben and me," I say.

"I know, but try not to worry about that today," Emily says.

"Morning guys, are you all excited?" Tilly walks in and puts her arm around Emily. "Are you okay?" she asks.

"Yes, although I wish you were there last night," Emily says.

"I'm sorry, I had a lot of paperwork to do," Tilly says.

"I had April with me so it was okay. But now you are both here, I have something to show you," Emily says.

She takes her phone out and we gather around.

Emily shows us a video of James and Paige having sex in what looks like the toilets in the coffee shop.

"Is that the coffee shop?" Tilly asks.

"Yes. I caught them last night when I was closing," Emily says.

"See, I told you," I say. "But he won't believe me," I say.

"He can't deny video proof, and I have a really good way to show it too, at the parade," Emily says and we shuffle closer to hear her plan.

◆ ◆ ◆

It's absolutely freezing. I change into my gold glittery playsuit and wrap my coat around me. Emily and Tilly also change for the parade. The crowds are already gathered and Ben's mum and dad, along with Victor, are putting up barriers all the way to the middle of the town centre as we drive to the town centre.

We arrive at the top of the hill, next to the town centre, where all of our floats are lined up. I get into my cake van with my cakes stored in a cupboard for the stops we are going to do. It's the first time I am going out for real in my van and I'm so excited.

The music starts. Song number one is Slade and we start our journey at one mile an hour as the dancers in front of us spin and sparkle in the now drizzle. The lights wrapped around each of the floats blur and sparkle and it feels amazingly festive. We wave to the crowds that have joined us and are following us along. Children are waving to Ben dressed as Santa, sat in his grotto-style chair. He has a microphone and is 'ho ho-hoing' to the crowds.

We make our first stop off and Neil and Dawn, dressed as elves, undo the barriers for the crowds to buy our cakes, coffee and the trinkets from Emily-who has been working hard making little souvenirs.

After I sell a few mince pies, the crowds begin following us again. I shut my little shutter and take a couple of minutes with the coffee Mum made for me. I'm so cold. The weather is freezing and the drizzle that began when we started moving is slowly turning into sleet. It hasn't discouraged the crowds who are all singing along to Mariah as we make our way past the college on our way to the village.

On our second stop, I keep my ice cream van closed

but come out with trays of Santa, elf and reindeer biscuits for the crowds. Mum follows behind me with coffee for everyone. The sleet isn't ruining anyone's time and we're all in high spirits. I'm buzzing by the time I reach Paige and Ben and I'm not letting them get to me.

"Biscuit guys?" I say politely to them. Paige doesn't even turn to face me.

"Yes please, thank you," Ben says and takes one. Mum hands them both a drink and nudges me on to the others. I reach Tilly's float with the children all dressed as the nativity scene.

"I'm so pleased to see you," Tilly says. The children all gather around for squash handed out by Mum and the teachers.

"Are you?" I ask.

"Yes, you are doing fantastic," Tilly says. Emily comes over and joins us. We envelope each other in a hug.

"I want to fill you in on the plan for Paige," Emily says when we pull away.

"So we have a huge stage that James is performing on and in between the sets you've organised school dancing, well, after that I am hooking up this video to the projector to show the whole village what Paige and James are doing. Surely after that Ben can't deny it," Emily says.

"That's fantastic," Tilly says.

"Yeah it is," I say, unsure of what it is I'm feeling. Do I want Ben to find out about Paige? I don't want him to get hurt. I don't like how I am feeling right now.

"Can all float owners get back on their floats please," Dawn shouts through a megaphone and we start moving again, just in time for Shakin' Stevens.

CHAPTER 22

We arrive in Birchlea-Heath village just outside the coffee shop for our last but one stop and then we all pile into the park.

When we finally reach the park, the crowds are already there.

I stop the ice cream van next to the children's playground that is completely empty. No one wants to go on a slide in December.

I open up the flap to my ice cream van and Paige is standing there, looking annoyed. She leans in. Luckily I have no customers.

"I told you to stay away from him," Paige says threateningly.

"You can't tell me who I can and can't talk to," I say.

Tilly and Emily are standing in front of Paige when she turns around.

"Don't threaten my sister or you will have me to deal with," Emily says

"I've seen the way you look at him and you two, do you really want me to tell the village what you are," she threatens. And wanders off.

I serve a customer and watch Paige walk across the field. Tilly and Emily are walking towards the stage.

I see Ben coming over. He hasn't seen Paige in the distance, and leans his elbow on my ledge when he gets to me. My heart flutters even after everything and I curse it. When will I stop feeling things for Ben?

"Hi, don't you have some Santa duties to do?" I ask, handing him a mince pie.

"No, I was only the float Santa, my dad has taken over now so I can enjoy my time. I want to say we make a good team. It was mostly you, I know, but I think we did something good," he says.

"We both did great organising the parade," I say.

"Before I go and find Paige, I just want to tell you that I meant it. I want to still be friends. I'm just not sure how to be your friend when Paige doesn't like you," he says.

"Ben, I thought we had done this before. I am not sneaking around being your friend," I say.

"April," he says.

"No, Ben, listen, I can't be your friend when your wife isn't around. That isn't how friendship works and I have way too much respect for myself for that. One day I am going to find someone who wants to be with me and will love me and maybe I will have to leave this village to find it but I will," I say.

"You had that and you dumped him remember?" Ben says.

"Yeah, have you wondered the reason I dumped him?" I say. I fold my arms angrily.

"I still don't believe you," Ben says.

"Ben, don't you dare come over here telling me you want to be friends when your fiancé has been ignoring me for the past few days. We can't be friends. I am not being your back up friend when everyone gets sick of your wife because I still have feelings for you, despite everything," I say.

He grabs my face and kisses me before I can react and it feels amazing. Time feels like it has stopped, but there is a nagging feeling inside me. And as we pull away Paige is standing there.

"Shit, I have really screwed everything up," he says and walks off. Paige follows him.

◆ ◆ ◆

The weather is making the sky look darker than it is. Most of the stalls are under gazebos. The stage is lit up with lights and James is singing Christmas songs badly with his band. They've just finished the last song on their set list.

Tilly and Emily go up on stage.

"Hello everyone, can I just say thank you everyone for helping make this parade amazing . One person particular, you have brought the village together and this is a Christmas parade we will never forget. Everyone, a round of applause to April!" There is a smattering through the crowd.

"The one other person who was supposed to help our April but backed out the week before because he spent most of the time with his fiancé. For every person who has been mean to April I hope you are all really ashamed of yourselves, April was telling the truth the entire time," Tilly slurs and I wonder how much she has drunk.

"Yes, Ben, your so-called best friend was telling the truth about your fiancé," Emily says.

Oh god. I close up my ice cream van, now that I'm completely out of cakes, and walk slowly over to the stage. I see Paige and Ben looking confused and he locks eyes with me.

"So you wanted proof Benji boy, here is your proof," Tilly says. "Proof number one," Tilly says through the microphone. "Paige cheating with her ex James."

A video comes up on the stage screen of Paige and James snogging and then a pile of clothes on the floor.

"And don't forget she isn't very nice to Ben's friends," Tilly says.

She shows the video from earlier of Paige threatening me and threatening to out Tilly and Emily. Emily takes Tilly's hand.

"You see, we aren't scared what you say about us," Emily says and I smile proudly at them. Paige is going redder and Ben looks furious.

"So Ben and people of Birchlea-Heath, observe these pictures and video of our lovely Paige," Tilly says, showing a video of Paige and James singing 'I want You Back' at karaoke.

"This is what has been going on between Paige and James," Emily says.

The crowds is silent and no one knows what to do.

I head to the stage and take the microphone. "I'm sorry you had to find out like this," I say.

I walk down the steps to where Tilly and Emily are.

"We told you we would sort it all out," Emily says.

"I love you guys. I can't believe you came out to the entire village," I say.

"Well we don't want to hide away any more. We aren't scared who knows," Tilly says.

"Oh god what about Ben?" I ask.

The villagers are all chanting and I see Paige running out of the park, crying. But Ben is nowhere to be seen.

My phone starts vibrating and I take it out my pocket. Tilly and Emily lean over me as I open a text from Ben.

"It's Ben," I say.

Meet me by the swings.

"Do you want me to come with you?" she asks.

"Ben isn't going to hurt me," I say.

"Okay, but let me know if you need me," Emily says.

"I don't think she will be there," I say.

I run over to the swings. Ben is sat with his back to me, his head down. Tilly and Emily wait nearby. I look up at them and they wave to me encouragingly.

I sit on the swing next to him, holding onto the metal bars. They're freezing. The sky is dark now and everywhere is lit up by fairy lights and streetlamps. I play with my hands nervously.

"You know I really thought I had got it right this time," Ben says, swinging lightly on the swing.

"I'm so sorry Ben, I know you didn't believe me, but isn't it best that you know?" I say softly.

He looks up at me and I see his face shinning in the street light on the path.

"I don't know," he says. His voice is low and shaky.

"I'm sorry nothing has worked out, Ben. I'm sorry you had to find out the way you did," I say. I want to reach out to him. He looks so vulnerable and it breaks my heart.

"Yeah that's right nothing has worked out for me has it? Me and you and now Paige, maybe it's just me. Maybe I am shit at relationships," he says. He is looking at me now and I see him trembling.

"No, I know. I'm sorry we didn't work out. I'm sorry that I left and I'm sorry Paige in the end was awful. I told you what she did but you wouldn't listen .I don't blame you for not believing me because well, I hated seeing you together," I say. My voice is trembling as well and I'm so cold.

"I feel like such a twat now, and the entire village knows my relationship issues. I was so desperate to be happy that I would let someone like that come into my life. How do you think that makes me feel, April?" His voice is still so calm. I feel nervous. I think I would rather he shout at me.

"Ben, I don't think you're a twat at all," I say.

"It's all because of you; everything I feel is because of you. I don't know why but even after twelve fucking years I'm not over you and it's fucked me up so badly that I let someone like that into my life," he says.

"Ben, I'm not over you and I admit I am still fucking crazy about you. It drove me mad every day, especially seeing you with a girlfriend," I say.

He shakes his head. "I told you how I felt about you and yet you still did this and embarrassed me in front of the entire village. I don't think I can forgive that, April. Consider me officially over you," he says and gets up to leave.

I let the tears fall. Emily and Tilly get me home. It's pitch black and drizzling heavier now. I reach the door, I am wet through. But none of it matters because I hurt the one person I love more than anything.

CHAPTER 23

The last time we broke up I felt things. Of course I did, but none of it was as hard as this. Last time I could push it down and concentrate on my job as a baker. This time it hits and it hits hard.

I wake up the next morning and immediately want to cover my head and hide. Do I have to face the world today? Everyone knows what Paige did and I have a feeling I might be blamed for it.

"Come on, we have to open the bakery," Emily says.

"I really don't want to," I say, putting the pillow over my head. I am so nervous in case I bump into Ben. Oh god Ben. I cringe when I think how much I hurt him. I know it was for his own good but knowing now that he doesn't like me has broken my heart again.

"You can't avoid the world forever. Ben will get over it one day," Emily says.

"Yeah but he hates me," I say.

"For now maybe, but imagine if he had married

her?" she asks.

I sit up because I did think of that. I thought about seeing her around the village every day. I imagine if they had got married. Would she still see James on the side? How would I cope seeing them holding hands around the village?

"Okay, go away and let me get dressed," I say shooing her out the room.

She leaves and I quickly get dressed. I really shouldn't let anyone make me feel bad. Today is the day I get back on track with my ice cream van. With this mind-set I feel much better when I come downstairs. Mum is in the kitchen.

"Morning love," she says. Dad kisses my cheek.

"Hi," I say, wondering what they thought of last night.

"Would you like a cuppa before you open the bakery? Your dad and I are going Christmas shopping, so we are leaving you two in charge," Mum says.

Dad flips his newspaper. "Look love, the parade made the paper."

"Great," I say feeling nervous.

Dad passes me the paper and I see buzz words like thrilling, Christmassy and magical with photos of Ben and me on our floats and in my ice cream van.

On the next side is a picture of Paige with a still

from one of the videos Tilly and Emily used.

"It's a shame Paige was a bad girl," Mum sighs.

"Yeah, such a shame," I say, not feeling up to my cup of tea any more.

"But you were right love, you saw through her. I am proud of you for standing up for what is right," Dad says.

"You did the right thing," Mum says and pulls me into an unexpected hug. I feel moved by their sentiment and start crying.

Dad gets up and we end up all hugging together.

"He will forgive you," Mum says. "He has been your best friend for so many years."

"Yeah but Mum, he hates me. I wrecked his relationship," I cry.

"He might be unhappy for now, but just you wait. He will come back when he realises the mistake he made," Mum says.

"It just doesn't feel like that for now," I say.

"Go and distract yourself at work. Have you called up the mum who gave you her number for the party?" Mum asks.

I shake my head, looking in the kitchen drawer to find the tiny piece of paper. Her son's birthday is very soon. Could I get myself ready in time?

I put it in my pocket. It wouldn't hurt to call her,

would it?

◆ ◆ ◆

Emily flicks all the switches on while I start baking cookies, bread and mince pies. The sky is still dark when Emily flips the closed sign to open and I take out the baked goods to cool down and decorate.

I have five minutes. I should call the mum and see if I can help with the party.

I dial the number and it rings.

"Hello?" she says.

"Hi, this is April. You gave me your card. I have the ice cream van," I say. I should have thought about what to say first.

"Hi April!" I am so pleased you got back to me. Are you still available?" she asks.

"Yes, I haven't got any bookings yet. I would be happy to be there for Harrison -what is it you want?" I ask. I get a pad of paper out from the cupboard.

"Great. Harrison is only five, and we're having ten of his friends over on the twenty-first of December. I was wondering if we can just have little Christmas cupcakes coming out of the van, and if there is any way we can have a candyfloss machine?" she asks.

"I can give it a whirl," I say, writing it all down.

"Great, so the theme is fairs. We are having fire-breathers, hook a duck, you know, that kind of thing. I was just wondering how much it would cost for you to be there to provide the cakes?" she asks.

"Well I haven't figured it all out yet, but I was thinking of doing a basic package where the children get cakes from the van and then a bigger package where the children can pick their cakes and help decorate them themselves for a little bit more money. I will let you know the prices in a couple of days if that's okay," I say.

"Fantastic, we would love the bigger package. The children would love to decorate their cakes. If you could let me know before Friday, then I will see you at ten am?" she says.

"Okay, let me know how long you want me for and I can work out how much," I say.

"No problem. I will send that in an email and you just send me an invoice," she says and we say our goodbyes.

My first booking. I can't believe I will be baking with children. I am so excited.

"What's made you so happy?" Emily asks, coming over. Brew and Chill is filling up already.

"I have my first booking for a birthday party on Friday," I say.

"Congratulations! Do you want to celebrate later?

We can go to the pub and get dressed up-you know, show the world you don't care about Ben and also celebrate the absolute boss you are," Emily says.

"You know what, yes, why not. It's nine days until Christmas, we might as well celebrate," I say.

I can't believe it's come by so fast. I haven't bought anyone anything. I don't even really know where to start. I haven't been around and I feel so guilty for it. I should spend more time with Emily and Mum and Dad because no one lives forever.

"Great, do you want Tilly to come or it just to be me and you? We can do shots, talk or cry, or swear if you want to," she says and I laugh.

"I don't want to swear about Ben, I wish the paper hadn't printed every detail about it all," I say

"Yeah, I saw. Customers have been commenting on it, and you know no one is mad at you," she says.

"Really?" I ask, looking out to the customers. I have been mostly in the back baking, trying to avoid the villagers.

"Can you cover my break? I'm busting for the loo," Emily says and I walk out of the back and behind the counter. No one is paying me any attention.

I sigh with relief. I'm not sure what I was expecting but it isn't this. Could it be true no one blames me?

"Hello April love, I am pleased to see you actually," Ben's mum says.

"Oh are you?" I ask nervously.

"Yes, I will have a gingerbread latte to take away. I want to say I'm a little bit upset how you and the girls handled last night. It could have been done more discreetly, poor Ben is refusing to leave the house at the moment. But I am also proud of you both for organising the parade. You made a great team and really showed your dedication to the village," she says.

I make her drink and the tears start to cloud my vision. I serve Ben's mum her latte and she sees how upset I am. She throws her arms around me. Why is she being so nice to me?

"Ben will get over it I promise, just give him a little time," she says and leaves.

I wipe my face. I don't think I have ever cried at work. Especially when I worked at Milly's. It was the best job I ever had. I sigh. I really hope I can get this cake van business up and running.

The rest of the day is quiet and, apart from a few comments about Paige and the weather, I haven't really seen anyone. I especially haven't seen Ben. Is he really refusing to leave his house? Should I text him? He made is quite clear last night that he doesn't want to know me. My phone starts buzzing in my pocket.

"Hello?"

CHAPTER 24

I spent all day baking for this late booking at the pub. Weirdly, Emily disappeared halfway throughout the day so I've been on my own.

I wipe the sweat off of my forehead. This has been the hardest thing I have ever done, but I finally wrap up the last of the éclairs on the table. Every table of the café is full of cakes and biscuits, mince pies and éclairs. The pay for this event is massive and it could really help me to save up for my own place.

No one will tell me why I am needed. I text Emily to see what time she wants to meet as I have an event that's been sprung on me early, but she doesn't message back.

I put everything in the storage in the ice cream van and lock up the coffee shop ready to go home and change.

Once home, I get changed into a black Christmas dress with tights and boots. I brush my hair and make sure I haven't got any flour or anything in it, then get my coat on.

I drive the short journey to the pub. All of the lights are off. What is going on? I park in the car park. The car park is buzzing with cars and I lock up the van.

I try the doors of the pub and they don't open. There's a note to say go around to the garden. I follow the pub around, let myself into the garden and try the door to go in. It opens.

When I walk in it's as if it is shut. Everything is on, all of the machines are on and the buzz from the fridges is on.

"Hello," I call, feeling like I've walked into the start of a horror film.

"Surprise," I hear and everyone jumps out at me. I see Emily and Tilly dressed up in Christmas dresses with snowmen on them and Santas. Neil and Dawn are sitting down at one of the tables.

Mum comes over and hugs me.

"I told you no one is mad at you," she whispers.

"Did you all know about this?" I ask, looking over at everyone.

"Yes," they all say.

Harry starts making drinks for everyone.

"Where do you want the cakes?" I ask.

"Just bring them in and put them on the table,"

Harry says.

Half of the village follow me outside. I unlock the van and they all pile into the tiny van, taking the trays of cakes and éclairs.

When we've finished there is a feast and everyone helps themselves.

"I don't really understand what any of this is for," I say, hugging everyone who comes over and thanks me for the parade.

"I would like to say a few words about my amazing best friend April. Now, she has only been back for just over two weeks but I absolutely love her. Let's raise a toast to April," Tilly says raising her glass. I take my glass off the bar and hold it up.

Tilly and Emily sit at a table with me.

"I can't believe you all did this," I say. I can't stop smiling. Everyone who has had one of my cakes or biscuits has asked me for my business card. Annoyingly, I haven't printed any but I definitely will. I have passed on my number for now so I am hoping throughout next year I will get some bookings.

"Would anyone like to do any Christmas karaoke today? We're setting it up in fifteen minutes," Harry says.

"What do you think? We could do some Mariah or Arianna?" Tilly asks.

"Yeah sounds good," I say.

"Harry, can we have another one of these please?" Emily asks.

"So how is everything with you two?" I ask. I've noticed they have their arms around each other and it's lovely to see.

"Everything is great. Even Mum apologised for how she reacted," Emily says.

"That's really good," I say nodding. "They've always supported us, even if our decisions weren't good ones," I say.

"To family," Emily says.

"Okay folks, the karaoke machine is all set up so get your names down. Tonight we are celebrating friendships and Christmas," Harry says through the microphone.

"Right, I will put us down. We can decide what we sing after," Tilly says.

Tilly leaves and Emily hugs me. "You know I love you sis," she says.

"Of course I do," I say. Emily always gets like this when she has had a couple of drinks.

"I want to marry Tilly," she says.

"Ooh exciting," I say and we clink our glasses.

"I'm not sure if it's too soon. I mean, we've only been together for two weeks but we've been friends for a lifetime," she says.

"Exactly, and if you know its right then sod what anyone else says," I say.

"We are down on the list. Do you girls have any idea what song you want to sing?" Tilly asks.

"Yes I do," Emily jumps in before I can say anything. I shrug when Tilly raises an eyebrow to me.

"Okay," she says.

"Is everyone ready to sing their hearts out? Whether you fancy yourself as a Celine or Madonna, we don't judge here, just sing your heart out. Just like our first karaoke volunteer. He has lived here all his life and just wants to sing to the girl he loves," Harry says.

Just then the lights go out.

I can't see anything in front of me but no one else seems to be bothered. The lights come back on at the back of the pub, lighting up the karaoke machine and the silhouette behind the microphone. Is that Ben?

I look to Tilly and Emily who shrug.

Ben picks the microphone off the stand and the song starts. It's our song. 'Merry Christmas' by Ed Sheran and Elton. The song that keeps coming on throughout my time back here. Ben is now singing it. I take a couple of steps forward and our eyes lock. My stomach swirls and I don't know what to say. Has he forgiven me?

I walk closer to him and he holds out his hand for me to join him. I do and all the lights come back on. Everyone claps along as we finish the song.

"You were amazing," I say softly. He takes my hands.

"Thank you," he says.

"So are you okay?" I ask.

"Yes, weirdly when I sobered up and thought about the whole thing I realised that you were right. You went about it completely wrong but I appreciate the sentiment. And my mum and dad gave me a kick up the arse," he says.

"I'm really glad you are here and I am so sorry for everything. God I am an awful friend," I say.

He shakes his head. "No you aren't, I have been an awful friend. I'm so sorry for everything."

"Me too," I say.

"I meant what I said though. I had so many feelings and it confused the heck out of me," he says.

I nod feeling tears in my eyes. "Me too and it hurt me so much when you said you didn't want to be friends and you didn't love me anymore."

"I only said that last part because I was angry. Do you still love me?" he asks

"Yes," I say in a whisper.

"Me too," he says.

We forget everyone else around us as we both lean in closer. Ben wraps his arms around me and we kiss. It's the best kind of kiss. As the music around us finishes, everyone else claps. I pull away from Ben and smile. This is it. I have everything I will ever need.

The End

THANK YOU

Thank you so much for taking the time to read my new book. I hope you have enjoyed it. If you would take a few moments I would really appreciate it if you left me a review.

Amazon

Goodreads

ALL ABOUT THE AUTHOR

Jodie lives in a small village in Solihull with her husband and two children. She loves nothing more than dancing around embarrassingly to 90s music and eating mint chocolate. Jodie enjoys reading and writing books full of romance and swoon-worthy fictional men.

SOCIAL MEDIA

To keep up to date with any news on my books or when I will be announcing my next book check out my social media.

Facebook group; Jodie Homer author

Instagram; Jodie_loves_books

Twitter @umbrellacafe

Threads Jodie_loves_books

Tiktok Jodie_loves_books

TRADEMARK ACKNOWLEDGEMENT

The Mobile Bakery at the Christmas Parade features the following trademarked items... The author acknowledges the trademarked status and trademark owners of the following wordmarks mentioned in this work of fiction.

People and songs

- Mary Berry
- Madonna
- Slade
- O Come Let Us Adore Him
- Celine Dion
- Shakin Stevens
- Nigella
- Mud. "Lonely This Christmas." Lonely This Christmas, RAK. 1974. CD

- Carey, Mariah. 'All I Want For Christmas Is You.' Merry Christmas. Columbia.1994. CD

- Crosby, Bing. "It's Beginning To Look A lot Like Christmas." Merry Christmas Bing Crosby, Decca Records, MCA Records, Geffen Records. 1951. CD

- Staples, Mavis. "Christmas Vacation." National Lampoon's Christmas Vacation Music Soundtrack. 1989. CD

- Sheran, Ed & John, Elton. "Merry Christmas." The Lockdown Sessions, Asylum, Atlantic. 2021. CD

- Grande, Arianna. "Santa Tell Me." Christmas Kisses, Christmas & Chill. Republic. 2014. CD

- Lewis, Leona. "One More Sleep." Christmas, with love. RCA, Syco. 2013. CD

- Sisqo, "Thong Song." Unleash The Dragon. Def Soul. 2000. CD

- Slade. "Merry Christmas Everybody." Merry Christmas Everybody. Polydor. 1973. CD

- NSYNC. "I Want You Back," NSYNC. RCA. 1997. CD

- Richie, Lionel & Ross, Diana. "Endless Love," Endless Love: Original Motion Picture Soundtrack. 1981.CD

- Dee, Kiki & John, Elton "Don't Go Breaking My Heart," 1976.

Rocket (UK)MCA (US). CD

- Kirsty MacColl, Shane, MacGowan. "Fairytale Of New York." If I Should Fall from Grace with God. 1987. Pogue Mohoney. CD

- Los del Rio. "Macarena." A mí me gusta and Fiesta Macarena. 1995. RCA. CD

Companies

- Nokia
- Range Rover
- Etsy
- Google
- BBC
- Coco Pops   Kellogg Company
- Coop
- Facebook: Meta Platforms, Inc
- Sourz: Sourz Drinks

Film and TV

- Rocky. Dir. John G. Avildsen. Perf. Sylvester Stallone, Talia Shire, Burt Young. Chartoff-Winkler Productions. 1976. Picture.

- Crane, D & Kauffman, M (Producers). (1994). Friends [Television series]. Burbank California: Warner Bros

- The Notebook. Dir. Nick Cassavetes. Perf. Ryan

Gosling, Rachel McAdams, James Garner. New Line Cinema, 2004. DVD

• The Grinch. Dir. Ron Howard. Perf. Jim Carrey, Jeffrey Tambor. Universal Pictures, 2000. DVD

• Titanic. Dir. James Cameron. Perf. Kate Winslet, Leonardo Dicaprio. Paramount Pictures, 20th Century Fox, Lightstorm Entertainment. 1997. DVD

• Andy Devonshire, Scott Tankard (producers/director The Great British Bake off. [Television series]. United Kingdom. Love Productions.

Events

• Macy Parade

MAGICAL CHRISTMAS ON THE ISLE OF SKYE - CHAPTER 1

The man on the TV is annoying.

"Our countdown begins in thirty minutes," he says, interrupting the news segment.

It's New Year's Eve-. Well, actually, it's half-past eleven on New Year's Eve and here I am, alone again. I was invited to my parents' pity party, but I didn't want to be the only one without a date. My friends are all out clubbing, but I have to admit, I'm at the higher end of my twenties and just can't be arsed with clubbing any more.

I put down my bottle of rosé and jumbo box of mince pies, a bargain that was knocked down from £3 to 50p and listen to the two people on the TV.

"We'll now say hello to our New Year psychic!" says Grant Holdman, the balding news anchor, who is sitting a little too snugly next to his guest star.

"Hello and Happy New Year." Mystic Alice looks like she has just stepped out of the 1500s. She's wearing old- fashioned style dress, with braided hair tied in ribbons.

"Lonely hearts of England, I want to hear from you. Have you recently broken up with someone?" I think her hypnotic voice has a slight Scottish accent to it. Unless I'm drunker than I thought.

"Whatever reason you're alone, give us a call," she says enthusiastically.

No. I can't. I shake my head, feeling ridiculous. What can this woman do for me?

I stare at the phone. Although maybe it would give me answers?

Woof.

"No, Rog." I say, and giggle and stroke the head of my little border collie Rog.

He's having none of it and nudges the phone. Giving in, I dial the number and nervously wait.

Roger gives me the side-eye from his little chair, obviously proud of himself.

The phone rings on the TV making me jump, and I realise just how drunk I am.

Maybe this wasn't a good idea after all.

"Well, well, Mystic Alice, it seems you have a

caller." Grant claps his hands, looking amused.

"Hello there." The voice echoes through the phone and TV simultaneously. I turn the TV volume down.

"Hi," I say.

"What's your name, my love?" she asks.

Before I can say anything sarcastic and tell her she can stick her stupid "powers" where the sun doesn't shine, I slur, "Emilia."

"And, Emilia, what can we help you with today?" Grant says, smirking. He's clearly enjoying my misery. I look at Rog, who now has his back to me. The shame.

"Well, I've been sleeping with my best friend," I say, and the TV image of Mystic

Alice silently nods for me to continue. "And I feel so confused. I don't know if I like him."

Alice's eyebrows furrow as she listens.

"Well, Alice, what do you make of that?" Grant asks. He is mocking me. I'm too drunk to care, although I know I will regret it in the morning.

"Emilia, you need to think about how you really feel about this person," she says and looks at me through the TV. It's like she can see inside my soul and a shiver goes up my spine.

"Do you want to be with him, or do you want to let him go? I want to know, do you have a history with this person?"

"Yes. No. I don't know... I'm so confused," I say. Regret slowly creeps over me like I'm being submerged in water.

"To save you going round and round in circles, tell them exactly what you've told me. You might be surprised," she says.

"Yes, well, that was an interesting phone call." Grant interrupts her and the phone line goes dead. They've already forgotten about me and are moving on to the next caller. I cringe as I think of what I've just told the entire country. What if my family and friends heard it? I think I need more wine.

Printed in Great Britain
by Amazon